"The intricate world, g~~rime, sk~~ of *The Lies of Locke Lamora* made newly intense and deliciously fraught by the emotional mastery of Foz Meadows. My heart rises, twists, and crunches precisely as they direct it to."
—Emma Mieko Candon, author of *The Archive Undying*

"With all the worldbuilding brilliance and political bite of *Arcane*, Foz Meadows's *Finding Echoes* will break your heart and piss you off while refusing to ever let you lose hope. I'm a bit smitten."
—Brent Lambert, author of *A Necessary Chaos*

"Tense and heart-wrenching, Meadows' novella spins a tale of heartbreak and betrayal woven through with incisive political commentary and a meditation on the realities of addiction. Navigating a gritty world teeming with secrets and strange magics, Snow and Gem reckon with whether it's possible to mend wounds between them which run years deep—or their society's divisions, as old as the walls which defined them."
—Laura R. Samotin, author of *The Sins on Their Bones*

"Meadows writes fascinating and sympathetic characters with believably complicated mutual histories moving through a vividly imagined city in collapse, in a fast-moving story which asks questions about responsibility, how change happens, and what we owe to one another. I raced through this thoroughly enjoyable book."
—Juliet Kemp, author of *The City Revealed*

"Intense, atmospheric, and full of heart."
—Joseph Brassey, author of *Skyfarer* and *Dragon Road*

Neon Hemlock Press
www.neonhemlock.com
@neonhemlock

Finding Echoes
Foz Meadows

Cover Illustration by Matthew Spencer
Cover Design and Layout by dave ring
Interior Design and Layout by dave ring
Edited by dave ring

Print ISBN-13: 978-1-952086-68-7
Ebook ISBN-13: 978-1-952086-78-6

Foz Meadows
FINDING ECHOES
Neon Hemlock Press

NEON HEMLOCK

FINDING ECHOES

A TALE OF NEW ARCADIA

BY FOZ MEADOWS

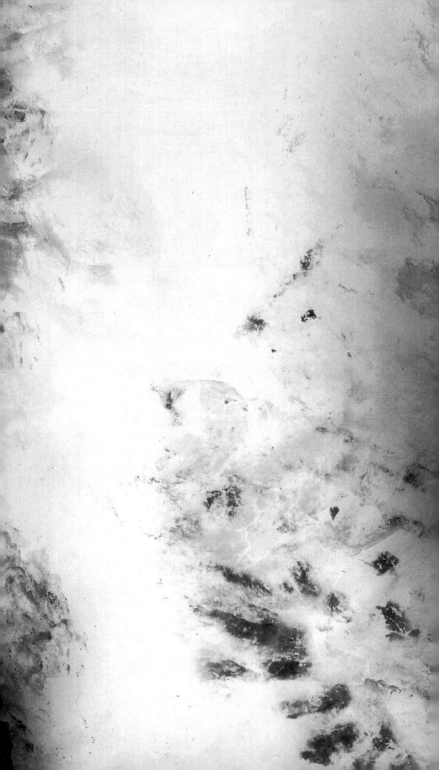

I

THE DEAD BOY'S umbra is three days faint, shot through with red and black. It crouches in the cramped and cluttered corner of this cramped and cluttered rookery, waiting for time or a vox like me to bring it some semblance of peace. Unlike the boy himself, the umbra bears no signs of violence, no cuts or blood or bruising. Its face is clear, its clothes as neat as they ever were in life. The Kithans would have me believe that what I see here is the soul of the boy whose body lies shrouded and cold three rooms away, poor minnow, but I don't believe that. People lie, but umbras can't: they're shadows of the dead, not the dead themselves.

The umbra whimpers: a high, thin note that I alone can hear.

"Mikas?" I say, kneeling. "Mikas, can you speak?"

Behind me, Rahina stifles a sob. "You see him, Snow? You see my boy?"

"I see him."

The umbra turns its ghostly head and looks at me with wide, unseeing eyes.

"Who killed you, Mikas?" I ask it—gently, for Rahina's sake. "How did you die?"

Uncle Tavo hit me, says the umbra. *He hit me and hit me. I fell down the stairs, and I stopped.*

I wince. I'd guessed as much, but there's no joy in hearing it proven.

I want to know why Tavo did it, but Mikas was too young for questions about adult motives. Instead I ask, "Was he angry?"

The umbra nods. *Really very.*

"Do you know why he was angry?"

Another nod. The umbra shivers like horseflesh twitching away a fly, which means I've little time left. This long unfound, I'm lucky to get anything at all.

I spilled his quartz, the umbra says, hunched up with remembered fear. *I didn't mean to. I'm sorry.*

My throat tightens. "Don't be sorry, Mikas. It's not your fault."

The umbra looks at me, opens its mouth, and dissolves in a shudder of static. Blown away like a dandelion blossom of stars and silence.

"Well?" says Rahina, voice trembling. "What did he say?"

I don't want to tell her. She won't want to hear it. But she asked me here for a purpose, and so I must.

When I stand, I look her in the eye. She's shorter than me, though I'm hardly tall: Charybdis-born, the both of us, as underfed and undergrown as Mikas was.

"Your brother did it," I say. "Mikas spilled his quartz, and Tavo knocked him down the stairs in a rage."

Rahina shudders, grabs the wall and keens with grief. I brace her shoulder and she falls against me, thin bones pressing hard under skinny muscle.

"I took him in to spare him the mines," she wails. "And he does *this*?"

There's lots of things I could try to say, but none of them would help. Ever since the Assembly ruled quartz use a crime in New Arcadia, it's even less safe for addicts to get help. Most aren't violent—quartz brings pleasure and dreamy stillness, not the sparkling energy of starbright— but from the little I know of Tavo, he's always tended to anger. Maybe that's what drew him to quartz, before choice became need: to escape his own actions. The sad truth is that addicts always have reasons, but regardless of what they are, Charybdis Precinct is full of their ghosts and the ghosts of those caught between drug and user—far too many for just one vox to dispel. But I do my best. I try, though I have no temple-training; no comforting lies about souls and ascendance to offer those left with grief.

I have only the truth of the dead, and the will to speak it.

Rahina cries, and I hold her. The room in which we stand is one of two her family rents, squalid and small and three doors over from where she lives with her husband, her two remaining children, and Tavo. This room belongs to her sister-in-law, with whose children Mikas often played. Right now, they're out roaming while their mother works—too young yet to be junza-jakes, but old enough to recognise what their future holds—but their absence didn't matter to Mikas's umbra. In death, his shadow knew only that this room, where a living boy once joked and laughed, was a place of safety, and so here it came.

Umbras can tell me how their bodies died, but they don't always know they're dead. Murder victims especially, those who die in pain and fear, are prone to fleeing their corpses, trying vainly to hide from what's already killed them. It makes it harder to bring them justice, assuming there's some to be had, but the dead don't know that, and telling them changes nothing.

If I were a shield of the city or a proper Kithan acolyte, as most voxes are, I'd carry a lancet and coil to record the umbra's final testimony in a form Rahina could see and hear.

Had she coin, she might even purchase a lyracite shard to hold a soundless image of her dead son, copied from my lancet's record. But this is Charybdis Precinct. Even a shard of lyracite is too lofty for someone like Rahina, while the wealth contained in a lancet and coil, if I ever acquired such tools, would paint a target on my back, regardless of junza politics. Instead, I trust that I am trusted to speak the truth, regardless of what it might cost me.

Regardless of what it costs the ones I tell.

Rahina doesn't call me a liar, doesn't ask me if I'm sure. She cries herself out against my shoulder, and when she pulls away to lead me from her sister-in-law's room, back to the rookery hall and into her own space, she does so in horrible silence.

Inside, we find Tavo right where we left him, skyed to the nines in the only available chair. Quartz has winnowed his big frame down to bone and sinew, leeching the natural colour from his hair, skin, eyes. Once, he was as brown as Rahina, good Deyosi stock; now his skin is mottled the strange, shiny grey of lead, his hair an unnatural white.

My hair is white, too, and the fingers of my left hand look dipped in silver, though I've never taken so much as a pinch of quartz. But my mother did, whoever she was, and her usage claimed me as her name never has. If Tavo ever weans himself clean, his natural colouring will likely revert, but my white-and-grey is permanent. At least the rest of me looks reasonably healthy, my skin a golden brown that's something other than Deyosi, or maybe a mix of somethings, if I guess by the mossy threads in my dark brown eyes, their single lids; the lack of curl to my hair. I don't know what I am, but I know what Tavo is.

He's not coming back from this.

Rahina stares in hopeless grief at her dead son's body, laid on the rickety table beneath a thin, patched sheet. She looks at her brother, twitching in his quartz-dreams, as oblivious to our presence as he is to his nephew's corpse.

"If I killed him for this," she asks, softly, "would you judge me?"

Perhaps I should wish that my answer was yes, but I've never been that noble. "No," I tell her.

Her fists clench. Almost, she looks like she's ready to act on it, here and now—and then she slumps, her shoulders bowing forward.

"I've no scrape to pay for burial," she says, looking back at Mikas, "and not the arms to carry him to the temple. Not alone."

She doesn't ask, but I answer anyway.

I help her lift her son.

AFTERWARDS, MY ARMS and shoulders aching from the unexpected labour, I meet Lark at the Hollow Star for a drink I badly need. She's already waiting, elbows propped on the cracked and greasy wood of our usual table as she nurses a pot of eyeblind. Her red hair gleams in even the dimmest light, and when she spots me, she grins, poking her tongue through the gap left by her missing front tooth.

"There he is!" she says, straightening as I seat myself opposite. "Kithani's tits, Snow, you look like curdled shit."

"I feel like it, too." I take a swallow of eyeblind, grimacing at the worse than usual burn.

Lark's face twists with sympathy. "Should I ask?"

"I'd prefer you didn't. Later, maybe."

"So noted." She taps her pot against mine. We drink together, silent against the usual grumbling chatter of the Hollow Star.

Mikas is not the first body I've carried to Ushai's temple, nor is he my first tragedy. I'm an outcast vox who talks to the dead in Charybdis Precinct: the ghosts I see belong to addicts, the elderly, to those dead of hunger and illness, to suicides and the victims of violent crime.

Most days, I can harden myself against it, but children…I don't ever want to be the sort of man who can shrug off a child's death.

I drain my pot faster than usual—faster, certainly, than I mean to. I stare at the empty cup, at a loss for what to do with it.

"Stay here," Lark says, kindly. "I'll fetch another."

I nod, not quite trusting myself to speak, and spend her brief absence mastering myself. By the time she comes back, I've determined to be better company, and prove as much by murmuring thanks when she hands me a fresh, cool pot.

"You know," she says, "if you need a break from Charybdis, I've got a job you might want to consider."

I stifle a groan. "Not another one of your fucking schemes, please—"

"Not mine, and not a scheme. Listen." She leans in, lowering her voice. "You've heard of the Red Steps?"

"Those anti-Assembly stoushers over in Argos?"

"Not just in Argos, but yeah, them." She sips her drink, brown eyes bright. "I know a fel as works with them in need of a vox's aid. He's clear desperate, Snow, and with good reason. And he can pay, too, real coin."

She pauses, waiting for my say-so. I sigh and flick my silver fingers. "All right. Tell me."

Lark grins. "Knew you'd see reason." She swigs from her pot, wipes her mouth on her hand and settles in. "So. Way this fel tells it, the Red Steps have been working sly for that progressive mawk in the Assembly, Vitho-whoever, hunting out proof the higher-ups in the Stonemetal Guild are in bed with the connexi, shilling quartz to their prison-gangs, 'cos half those crews are in for addict-crimes anyway, and they die too soon to be useful if they're taken straight off the white. Need to string 'em along a bit, yeah? Give 'em just enough to keep going, but not so much they're too skyed to work. And of course, when the guards there 'find' 'em using, they get time added to their sentences, which means more free labour and less shifts going to miners as actually earn a wage."

"Fucking goldplates," I mutter.

"Fucking goldplates," Lark agrees. "So, a noble cause. But their shattersnipe ain't come back."

I see where this is going. "So they think he's dead, and they want me to speak his umbra, find out what got him killed and why?"

"Exactly," says Lark. "Only thing is, they ain't got a body. My fel's the one tasked with finding it, and given it's been a day already and where they've got to look, he figures he needs a vox in hand or else they won't get the ghost in time."

I stare at Lark. "So, what—he wants to smuggle me into the lyracite mines to help look for a body and hope we don't get caught? That's the plan?"

"That's the plan."

"Fuck." I stare at the filthy roof and down a swallow of eyeblind. If it weren't for the city's many walls, you could see the hills that mark the mines from any decent vantage point. But the walls are older than New Arcadia: a legacy of long ago, when the city was known as Jerichae, whose denizens must've built them for a reason. Ancient history, except that it binds us still. "That's *worse* than one of your schemes, Lark. Signing on with the Red Steps is bad enough, but trying to fox the Stonemetal Guild for some fucking Assemblyman? If I wanted to die that badly, I'd just lie down and do it."

"Maybe so," Lark says, softly. "But time was, you wanted something to live for, too. Isn't a better city worth fighting for?"

The blow lands square as a stousher's hook. My mouth goes numb. I want to throw my drink at her, but Lark holds my gaze in a way that says she already knows I'm going to help; that she likely knew before I ever walked in.

"Gods damn you," I whisper. "Gods *fucking* damn you, Larkspur."

She snorts. "You don't believe in the gods."

"But you do." I pause, letting my lip curl. "Even if they haven't always returned the favour."

Now it's her turn to take a hit. She glares at me, fierce and wounded. Lark was an acolyte, once; and technically she's still temple-sworn, claimed by the Kithans in some nitpick way that lets her pass between precincts as freely as I do between junzas, but she hates to admit the particulars.

She glares at me. "I suppose I deserved that." She drains her pot, thumps it crossly on the table, then breathes in big and flashes me her scheming smile. "Well, then. Want to meet him?"

I startle. "What, now?"

"Yes, now." She pulls a face. "Lacksakes, Snow, I *told* you it was urgent. He wants quiet to meet, or I'dve brought him here. He's back at my stoop, waiting."

"You trust him enough to leave him there alone?"

"I trust him," Lark says, "same as I trust you." She makes a hurry-up motion, gesturing at my unfinished pot. "Let's go already!"

"And what would you have done if I'd said no?" I ask, just to be petty. I love Lark, but sometimes I hate that she knows me so well. In answer, she shoots me a withering look and mimes drinking, so I roll my eyes, finish my pot and follow her onto the street.

Late afternoon sunlight clings to the greys and browns of Charybdis Precinct like dripping treacle, making what's hard seem soft. The Hollow Star sits in the middle district, squeezed between the junza-territories of the Dark Heart and the almost-reputable squalor of the rookeries where Rahina's family lives, among so many others. I shove the thought away and focus on the present, walking quickstep alongside Lark, hood drawn up to hide my quartzborn hair. Not that I take glib for it—not here, not with so many addicts and the children of addicts going about their business—but I'm known in Charybdis, and I'd rather not be flagged down on the way to Lark's meet-see.

Lark lives in two small rooms above a mender's shop on Cant Street. She unlocks the door to the rickety inner stair with a key on her necklace, ushers me ahead of her as she locks up behind us, then pushes past on the landing to unlock her place in turn.

"In," she says, shoving me forwards.

I step inside, and see who's waiting, and freeze.

The man is my age, tall and lean-boned under hard-won muscle. His shock of black hair is loose to his scarred and stubbled jaw, looped messily behind notched ears. His black eyes widen as he sees me, brown skin going ashy-pale. It's been eight years, but I'd know him anywhere, just as surely as he knows me.

"Ushai's grace," he whispers. "*Snow?*"

I nod, struck dumb. I take a step forwards, as does he, until there's less than an arm's reach between us. We were the same height once, but now I only come up to his chin. I'm trembling. I want to scream or fling myself at him, I don't know which. Flee, maybe, or touch him, just to prove that he's real.

I make myself speak, and my voice comes out as wet and raw as a new-shucked oyster. "*Gem?*"

Lark frowns in confusion, glancing between us. "You know each other?"

"Knew," says Gem, *my* Gem, who is here and whole and somehow still alive. He swallows hard, hand twitching as if to reach for me, too. "I thought you were dead," he says. "I thought—"

He doesn't finish the sentence, but he doesn't need to. I know what he wants to say.

I thought I killed you.

❧ II ❧

WE SIT AT Lark's table, sipping kaveel from her crooked clay mugs, and do not speak of the gulf of years that hangs between Gem and me.

"I need to find Reeve," he says, in a voice that only shakes if you know what to listen for. His accent is different, Charybdis vowels patched over with bits of Argos and Virgil, but I still hear their hitch beneath the gloss, like a different kind of ghost. His voice was always deep, but it's deeper now with age and secrets, fathomless as the Dio's dark water. "Dead or alive, he's our best chance at proving corruption in the Guild, and we need to show what's going on before the next elections, or Assemblyman Vitho and the progressives won't stand a chance."

"I don't carry a vox's kit," I say, the words strangely rote. "If your fel is dead and you want a recording, you'll need to bring tools—"

"I did," says Gem, and reaches into a battered leather satchel, pulling out a gleaming lancet and coil.

The breath snags in my throat; even Lark looks stunned. A small fortune sits before us, the lancet's sharp edges framed in the same soft brass that forms the coil's handle. The slender, triple-braided wand of lyracite, glass and copper tempts my fingers, molten in the honeyed light. I reach out and touch the lancet instead, shuddering to feel the thrum of my vox's gift echoed in pristine metal.

"This is brand new," I say to Gem, my eyes not leaving his. "Unused."

"It is," he says. "Don't ask how I got it."

"I wasn't going to."

Gem looks away, returning both tools to the satchel. "Reeve knew he might not come back from this. He told us not to come after him if it came to that, not to risk anyone else, but he'd do the same for me, and it's too important not to try in any case."

Lark opens her mouth, doubtless to say something intelligent, but my own dumb tongue gets in first. "You sound different," I blurt. "Your accent's gone. Mostly, anyway."

Gem flinches, palms pressed flat. "I grew up," he says, roughly. "I learned."

Where? I want to ask, and *Who from?* "Me, too," I say instead.

Lark coughs, startling both of us. "I'm not asking," she says, raising a pointed eyebrow, "but is whatever it is I'm not asking about going to be a problem?"

"No," we say in unison.

"Good," she says. "Now, as to payment—"

I tune out the practicalities. I usually do, if I'm honest, and for far worse reasons than the one now sitting opposite. Gem, my Gem, but not mine anymore. We've been dead to each other for eight whole years; the only soul I ever mourned more was Sohlan, and he raised me. Did Gem mourn me, too? He looks at me like I look at ghosts, his eyes like lyracite.

Lark strikes her bargain: a percentage of whatever Gem
and the Red Steps are paying me for this foolery, the exact
amount dependent on the outcome, plus a flat facilitator's
fee. Gem pays in hard coin drawn from the same satchel
as the vox's kit, and I marvel at the brass of him, to walk
through Charybdis carrying such riches. Not that the rest of
him reads as goldplate: he's dressed like a labourer in sturdy
boots, black kilted pants, a woven belt and a loose shirt the
colour of charcoal, its long sleeves cinched at the wrists.

"Do we go now, then?" I ask him, though I'm already
sure of the answer.

"We do." He glances at Lark, fiddling absently with his
satchel-strap. He seems on the brink of saying something,
but shakes his head and stands instead, pulling the satchel
onto his shoulder. I copy him without a thought, for all
that I can't quite believe he's here; that we're actually
doing this. It shouldn't be possible that some part of me
has always been waiting for Gem to come back, and yet
that's how it feels: as though he never left me, let alone to
Tamek's untender mercies.

"Luck to you both," says Lark. She stands and hugs me,
quick and tight, and presses a kiss to my cheek.

"Luck to you, too," I murmur.

She sees us all the way out, unlocking the street door
in silence. The sun has dipped below the walls now, only
faint light limning the tops of buildings. Twilight seeps
into the city's bones like creeping moss, the night air sharp
with the river's scent and the distant tang of industry.

I pull my hood back up and stare at the street, watching
as a ragged minnow scurries about to light such public
lamps as ever stay lit in Charybdis. "Where to?"

"Argos Precinct," Gem says. "We need to retrace
Reeve's steps, and that's where he started."

We walk. My short, fast stride is somehow a perfect
match for Gem's slow lope. I try not to look at him too
much, and almost certainly fail.

"I assume you have a plan for getting me past the gate guards after curfew?"

I feel more than see Gem startle. "You don't have a gatepass?"

"I'm quartzborn and unregistered, Gem. Of course I don't have a fucking gatepass."

"Not even a fake?"

"Not even a fake." I'm too clearly quartzborn for any Charybdis guard to leave me be; I've jumped the walls before, but not on a whim and never easily. I grit my teeth. "Does this mean you don't have a plan, then?"

He's fallen a beat behind my pace; his footsteps tap out of sync as he catches up. "No, I have a plan. The Red Steps have a safehouse here, on the rookery edge. We go there, get a pass and some dye for your hair, then through to Argos." He hesitates, then asks, "Y'ever been to Argos?"

His old Charybdis accent bleeds into the words, and something in me twists. We turn a corner, picking a path down Eyelet Row, where light and muted laughter spill from grimy jinshop windows.

"No," I tell him, tracking the nearby scuttle of an alley-rat. "Virgil once or twice, but never further."

"Truly?"

"Truly."

Another turning takes us onto Weaver Street, its shopfronts closed and shuttered. There are few lights here, and though the moons are visible, they're yet too dim to be of use. Gem slows, less sure of his footing than me. A petty part of me wants to let him flounder, but I slow my step and keep beside him, guiding us both by memory.

"What became of Tamek?" he asks, suddenly.

I stumble over nothing.

"I know he's dead," Gem says, voice faltering, "but not how, or when. I just wondered, is all."

Anger stirs in me. I keep my voice calm. "You never kept track of the junzas?"

"Not when I first left. Not for years." He laughs bitterly. "Outside Charybdis, they're not much spoken about beyond the rookery vote, the dayworkers in Argos and Virgil. Folks know the Dark Heart exists, they know of the junzas, but otherwise...well. It doesn't cross the precinct walls, or not enough to matter, so why should their worries?"

"Quartz crosses the walls," I snap. "So do the shields and the temples. So does trade. Why not care for criminals?"

"You know why," he says, and I hate that I do.

"Gem—"

"Wait." He grabs my arm, slowing the both of us. It's the first time he's touched me in eight full years; his palm is a brand through my shirt. Quietly, he asks, "Did you hear that?"

I cock my head, listening. Nothing unusual at first, then— there. A faint, scuffing footstep somewhere behind us. It slows as we do, picking up again when we quicken our pace.

Someone's foxing us. I swallow and nod.

"I hear it," I murmur. "Keep walking."

Gem obeys, though his hand doesn't leave my arm. The footsteps sound louder now, or maybe it's just that I've noticed them. I reach up and flip my hood off, baring my hair. Gem makes a questioning noise in his throat.

"The local jakes and jossers know to leave me be," I tell him, steering towards the next turning. "If they don't back off, it'll mean they're after you."

"I already assumed they were," Gem mutters. "Why would—"

Someone leaps out from around the corner, stabbing down with a blade that catches just enough light that I see it in time. I shout and backstep, the sharp point ripping a shallow cut down my chest instead of striking deep. It stings and burns; I hiss at the pain. Snarling, Gem shoves me out of the way and draws a knife from a sheath beneath his shirt. I stumble, dripping blood as he squares off with the striker, a hard-eyed woman with thin brown hair.

Footsteps speed past me in the dark, and I realise too late what's happening.

"'Ware behind!" I shout, and that's all the warning Gem gets before our fox, a skinny bald man, lunges at his blind spot with a rapier.

Swearing, scuffing; the scrape of metal on metal. I duck to the ground, heart hammering as I reach for the shockjack strapped to my calf. It's been a livelong since I've needed it, but junza protections or not, only a mawk walks unarmed here. I straighten just in time to see Gem catch the fox's blade with his own as the woman, sent sprawling, starts to rise.

Time moves slow. I raise the shockjack, bare my teeth and smash it down hard on the fox's neck. Electricity surges to life, a bone-deep buzz I feel secondhand. The fox spasms, gargles and drops like meat. Gem grins at me in the darkness, and for a second it's like we're jakes again, stoushing for Bonebreak honour on the junza's edge.

And then the striker surges upwards, faster than Gem can turn to block, and sticks him through the ribs.

A furious noise rips out of me. I'm on her as she yanks her blade out, whipping my shockjack hard into her face. She lets out a garbled cry and falls; I'd hit her again, but Gem is going to his knees, and I turn and catch him instead.

"Fuck," he gasps. My hand presses his where it covers the wound. His knuckles are slippery with blood, and a terrible calm descends on me. I'm not going to lose him again; not now, and certainly not like this, before I've even had the space in which to be properly angry at him. *Think!* I goad myself. *Think!*

"Get up," I rasp, looping an arm around his waist. I press our hands to his wound and take his weight, awkwardly shoving my shockjack into his satchel with blood-slippy fingers. "We need to go, now. Can you walk?"

Gem hisses and staggers. He leans on me but doesn't fall. "I'll manage," he grits out.

I leave our strikers where they lie; assuming I haven't killed them both, they won't be rising anytime soon. But where to go? Lark's place is close, but even if she's still at home, she's no healer. The nearest temple might help us, but they'd ask questions, and they're way at the other end of the middle district.

Which leaves only one option.

Swearing under my breath, I try to keep Gem's blood in him and steer us towards the Dark Heart of Charybdis Precinct.

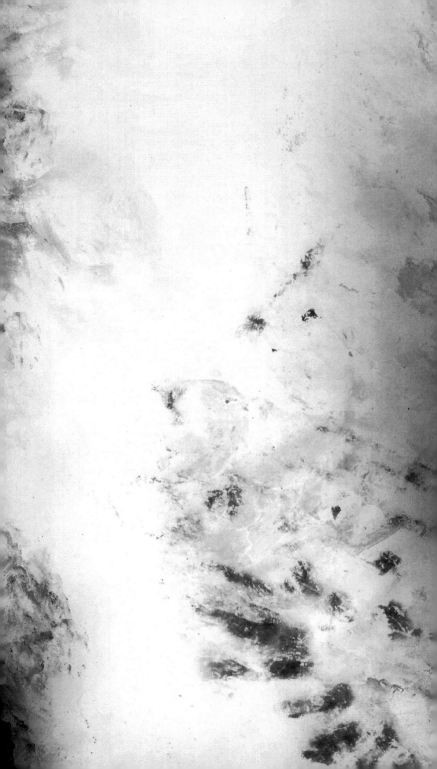

III

I BANG ON the door with a bloodied fist, my throat and lungs burning. "Emani! Emani, it's Snow! Let me in!"

Gem sags against me, pale with blood loss. He's sweaty and shaking, terrifyingly close to deadweight after our frantic, limping run through the precinct's maze.

"Snow," he croaks softly—the first thing he's said in nearly ten minutes. "Snow, I'm so sorry—"

"Don't you *dare*," I hiss at him, and pound on the door anew. "*Emani Kouta!*"

Footsteps from inside. A heavy lock clicks. The door cracks open, revealing a scowling woman with eyes like flint.

"Snow Kidama," Emani says, acidly. "What the fuck do you want?"

"Healing," I gasp, and barge our way into her house. She steps back, startled. We make it two paces past the threshold before Gem's knees give out, and I buckle with him, reflexively snatching his satchel into my lap. Her expression changes, anger replaced by calculation. She squats down,

looking Gem over with a practiced eye. She clucks her teeth
as she sees the wound, prising up his shirt where blood has
stuck it in place, and puts a hand to his side. Her rescari's
gift glows pale beneath his skin as she maps the damage.

"He's lost a lot of blood," she murmurs, "but his organs
and lungs are whole. I can fix him." She pulls her hand
back, gaze flicking over the cut on my chest. "You want
me to look at that, too?"

"It can wait," I say. "Him first."

"Suit yourself." She sits back on her knees and calls out,
"Hoi, Jeth!"

Her second son pokes his head into the main room.
"Yeah, ma?"

"Come lift this fel up on the cot." She stands, pushing
her sleeves to her elbows. To me, she says, "You, stay
where you are. I don't trust you to roam about."

I do as she says, if only because I'm too weary to do
otherwise. As Emani vanishes into the kitchen, Jeth rolls
his eyes and scoops Gem up as effortlessly as I lifted
Mikas. He's a big man by any standards, but doubly so for
one born and raised in the Dark Heart—but then, rescari
are valuable enough that their families seldom starve.
With a nod to me, Jeth lays Gem down on the healer's
cot that sits against the far wall, grunts at Gem's croaking
thanks, and then retreats to the doorway.

A moment later, Emani returns with a bottle of
eyeblind. She nods approvingly at Jeth, and only then
does he lumber away, heading up the stairs to the second
floor, another luxury earned by Emani's skills.

"Here," says Emani, thrusting the eyeblind at me.
"Pour that on your scratch, if you won't take healing; it'll
kill the foulness until I can look at it."

I do as she tells me, hissing through my teeth at the
sting and then sneaking a swig to deaden it. Recorking
the bottle, I knee-walk closer to the cot, where Emani has
pulled up a stool and sits at Gem's side.

"Don't fight me," she warns him, pushing his shirt up.

He shakes his head weakly. "I won't."

"Good." She sets her hands on his torso, one above and one below the wound, still bleeding sluggishly around a dark, clotted crust. I've witnessed far worse injuries, but this one is harder than most. I swallow, trembling slightly. Emani sets to work, eyes lambent with the bloodpink glow of her gift, and I force myself to bear witness.

Gem groans and twitches, but otherwise stays still. I can't remember the last time I watched a rescari heal; I've surely seen Emani work before, but the only images in my head are of Sohlan, who had my raising.

Sohlan, who fixed what Gem left of me.

The memory doesn't help; I shove it away and look at this older, newfound Gem in front of me, his breath coming slow and even now that he's not being forced to run. His eyes are half-lidded, his face lax under Emani's ministrations. The boy I knew couldn't grow a beard, but this Gem's jaw is dark with what would be a week's growth on me, the black hair flecked with white around an old scar. His face has filled into an adult shape; there are marks on him whose history I don't know, though his notched ears haven't changed. He's Gem and not-Gem, my memories transformed into a man who isn't quite a stranger.

I nearly lost him again.

I hug the satchel and look away, refusing the temptation of Emani's eyeblind. Whatever comes next, I'll need to be sober for it.

As Emani heals, I lean my back against the wall and settle in to wait. I ought to think about what I'm doing, how zamfool dangerous this is, but I'm not that clever. I let my thoughts empty out instead, let my breathing slow and my eyes slip shut, until the tension that's knotted into muscle and sinew forgets its reasons for being there and dissipates like mist. I put away all I have that hurts—the slash on my chest, Gem's everything, the heft of Mikas in my arms—and do nothing but sit, and breathe, and be, until I'm only a rhythm of breath and blood.

Time passes, and then—

"It's done," Emani says.

I startle, unsure how long it's been—less than an hour, I'd guess, based on Sohlan's old teaching of rescari limits—and scramble to kneel at the foot of the cot. Emani pushes back on her stool, looking pleased with herself as Gem stirs into wakefulness. Deep healing disorients most people, especially on top of trauma. Eyes unfocussed, he blinks and murmurs sleepily, "Reeve?"

The hope in his voice is a different sort of blade.

Oh.

"Not Reeve," I tell him, shoving down hard on a sick, incongruous twist of pain. "Snow."

"*Snow?*" he asks, disbelieving—and then, more lucidly, "Oh. Right."

He sits up, rubbing his head. He glances at me, a faint look of embarrassment on his face, then turns his attention to his now-closed wound, probing the tender skin with his fingertips. The scar is nearly two fingers wide, shiny pale and knotty at the edges.

"Thank you," he says to Emani. And then to me, a little more awkwardly, "Thank you, too."

Emani cackles. "I didn't do it for free, boy. Now." She crooks an impatient finger at me. "You going to let me fix that scrape? Can't have the bosses' darling all marked up."

Gem shoots me a sharp look at that, but there's no point arguing even if I wanted to. I sit myself at Emani's feet and shiver as she sets a hand to my chest. Her gift hums through me, an itching tickle that makes my teeth buzz. Within minutes, the scratch is scabbed over; Emani makes a satisfied noise and motions for me to pass her the eyeblind. I do so, and she takes a long draught of it, wiping her mouth on her shirt.

"Well, now," she says, when she's drunk her fill. She flicks her gaze between us. "You want to tell me what happened?"

"It's better if we don't," I say, as Gem opens his mouth. "What do I owe you?"

Emani makes a show of considering. "I ought to say an imp, just for the inconvenience." Gem goggles at that, though sensibly keeps his mouth shut. "But as it's you, Snow, I'll settle for ten knaves."

"Five," I counter. It's bad manners not to haggle.

"Eight."

"Six."

"Done."

We double-knock the backs of our left hands to seal the bargain.

"Guessing you've not got it on you?" Emani says. I shoot her a look that says *of course not*, and she heaves a theatrical sigh. "I oughta charge you extra for the wait, Snow. I'm getting soft."

"Never." And then, because she's still looking expectant, I add, "I'll have it to you within the week, or you can bring it up with Savu. My word on it."

"Your word." Emani makes a face. "That's good for something, I suppose." She stands and stretches, flapping a hand at Gem to get him off the cot. He rises, only a little unsteady, and extends a hand to me. Rather than take it, I pass up his satchel and roll to my feet.

"Thank you," I say to Emani, offering her a bow.

Emani's expression does something I can't interpret. "Don't thank me yet," she says, and I'm halfway to asking what that means when there's a thump on her front door. Emani goes to answer it without meeting my gaze, which ought to clue me in, and yet I'm still shocked when she opens it to reveal her daughter, Kisi, accompanied by no less than four of Savu's jakes, distinguished as such by the green bands tied to their forearms.

A skinny girl of eight, Kisi runs straight to her mother's side and stays there, grinning at me with all the accomplished mischief of one born to the junzas.

I remember how long it took Emani to open the door for me and Gem, and groan at the belated realisation that she sent Kisi running for Savu before we'd even crossed the threshold. I curse myself for a mawk; there's a *reason* I thought that bringing Gem here was a risk, but Emani seemed so calm that I let myself forget it.

"Sorry, Snow," says Emani, in a tone that says she's not sorry at all. "You know how it is."

I don't answer that, because I do. One of the jakes steps in as Gem moves alongside me, assessing us both. I stifle a curse: it's Nixa, one of Savu's trusted hands. Her brown eyes narrow as she sights the fresh scar on my chest, then widen again as she clocks Gem, a look of puzzlement crossing her face.

"I know you," she says, with just a hint of question. She prowls over to us, taking in his bloodied clothes, his height. She stares at the notches in his ears, frowning in confusion, and for half a moment I think she'll let the mystery rest. Nixa is our age, but she was never Tamek's; she's only ever run with the Scapegrace crew. But then it clicks, and I see the knowledge roll over her like a fogbank cresting the walls.

"Yuhiqa's bloody clutch," she breathes. "You're Gem the Diamond. Gem the fucking Diamond!"

Gem freezes in place. Emani inhales, sharp and shocked, while the jakes on the doorstep murmur incredulously.

Nixa lets out a burst of wild laughter that fades the longer she looks at me. Her smile falls, untwisting the scar that jags across the brownblack skin of her left cheek. She's all over too dark to be truly quartzborn, but there's streaks of white enough in her kinky, coiled hair that we've always had some kinship, which maybe explains the sympathy in her eyes.

"Oh, Snow," she says, sadly. "What a fucking mess, eh?" She sighs. "I've gotta take you to Savu. You *know* that, I'll catch teeth if I don't."

"*What?*" says Gem, jerking out of his stupor. To me, he hisses, "We need to get going——"

"Don't," I say. It comes out ugly, and Gem stills all over again. I swallow around a burst of anger and say, more calmly, "It can't be helped. We're in Savu's junza, which makes us her business. But me and her, we're… we understand each other. It'll be fine, so long as we go quietly."

"Smart fel, this one," says Nixa. "Come on, then."

Gem looks at me imploringly. "Snow——"

"We don't have a choice."

As Emani and Kisi look on, I take Gem's arm and pull him out the door. Nixa follows us, and without so much as a word exchanged, she and her jakes form up like an honour guard, marching us on to Savu's court.

Gem turns his head as we reach the corner, watching Emani's house disappear from view. When he finally speaks again, his voice is carefully neutral.

"This is the Scapegrace junza now?"

"It is."

"What happened to Bonebreak?"

"It doesn't exist anymore."

Gem stares at me in the darkness. "You never answered me, before."

"Answered what?"

"About Tamek. What happened to him?"

My pulse ticks up, and the listening jakes all chuckle. Gem frowns at them. "What's funny?"

"Snow happened to Tamek," Nixa says witheringly. "Everyone knows that."

Softly, Gem says, "I didn't."

❧ IV ❧

A HALF-HOUR MARCH through the Dark Heart sees us safe to Savu's court: a repurposed warehouse set in a courtyard that once held wagons and is now home to an endless rotation of jakes. Fires burn in braziers placed at intervals across the cracked paving, ringed by armed and tattered figures. The clink of bottles, faint strains of music, and an undercurrent of laughter all conspire to mock the fledgling night.

Gem hasn't spoken to me since he asked about Tamek, nor have I spoken to him, but he breaks that silence now.

"Here?" he whispers. "Still?"

I bite back a curse. Savu's court was Tamek's, once. Before today, this was the last place Gem and I ever saw each other, and while I've had the better part of a decade's comings and goings to soothe that bleak association, Gem has not.

"It's all right," I murmur back. It's an obvious lie, and Gem rightly glares at me for it. Even so, we draw closer to one another as Nixa leads us over the threshold, little rifts of silence forming as we pass each fire and filling again in our wake.

The man standing guard at the court's doors relaxes as he sees us approach, cocking a thumb at the court.

"She's waiting for you," he says to Nixa, his voice a low rumble. He gives me a nod, but casts a pointed glance at Gem's satchel. "Need to check that."

Gem pales. When he hesitates, Nixa huffs impatiently and grabs it from him, forcing Gem into an awkward lean as she tugs the strap over his head.

"Let me," she says, opening the flap. She finds my bloody shockjack first, of course, and rolls her eyes as she throws it to me. Gem looks startled at that, but it's not really the moment to explain why Savu's jakes know what weapon I carry, and so I crouch down, returning it to its holster.

When I straighten again, both Nixa and the guard are staring at the lancet and coil with twin expressions of greedy shock. I swallow, hard.

"We need that, Nixa," I say, a little desperately.

"We all need a lot of things," she replies. She spares a final glance for the lancet, stroking the edge with a fingertip, then shuts the bag and snugs it against her chest. The guard opens the door, and Nixa waves the pair of us through, still flanked by the other jakes.

We enter a jackdaw-furnished space overhung by half of a second, more private level. Once it was where the warehouse overseers wrote and counted; now, it's where Savu and her most trusted live. But Savu's not hidden away up there: she's holding court, lounging decadent on her salvaged throne, one leg thrown over the armrest and a foot pressed firm to the floor. The music we heard faintly outside is loud in here, its source a trio of jakes possessed of drum, kitar and voice. All three seem lost in their playing,

but as we draw close to Savu's throne, she waves them into
silence and they comply without hesitation. Heads turn our
way at the interruption. Conversation dies.

With slow and powerful theatre, Savu Scapegrace sits
upright, her raised leg swinging down. She greets us with
a not-quite-smile: her teeth are filed sharp, with three
replaced by gleaming metal duplicates. Her kinky hair
is twisted up in a crown of coiled knots, a high collar
of carved jade panels snug around her throat. A green
dragon tattoo snakes around her left forearm, while her
right is shiny with old burn scars, the kind that never
knew a rescari's touch.

Nixa goes to one knee before her, as do the other three
jakes. I copy a beat behind them, and Gem a beat behind
me, until all of us bow in the shadow of Savu's power.

"I've brought you Snow Kidama, boss," says Nixa,
when Savu waves her up again. "And with him, Gem the
Diamond."

A ripple of shock runs through the room, as well it
might. Savu raises a twice-scarred brow and gestures for
us to rise, too. I scramble up, but Gem doesn't move. I
nudge him, and he startles as if from a stupor, lurching to
his feet. He's unsteady enough that I almost reach to hold
his arm.

"Gem the Diamond? Truly?" Savu asks. Her rich voice
fills the room like smoke.

"Truly," Gem rasps.

Savu looks him over. "We thought you were dead."

Gem clasps his hands behind his back, an old trick to
still his fidgeting. "I wasn't."

"Clearly," says Savu. She looks at me, her amber gaze
sharp. "You were attacked in the middle district. Injured,
Kisi said."

It's not a question. I nod, mouth dry, the implications only
belatedly sinking in. Lacksakes, where are my wits tonight?
"A passing scratch," I say. "It was outside the junza—"

"The peace is the peace," says Savu, voice hard. "I will not have it broken. Who attacked you? Why? Where are they now?"

I glance at Gem, not sure how much of our purpose he wants to conceal, yet knowing bone-deep that lying outright to Savu is not an option.

Gem squares himself. "We were attacked on my account," he says. "Trouble with rivals in Argos; I thought I'd left it behind, but they followed me here. We left them where they fell." He hesitates, then adds, "Snow shockjacked them."

Savu laughs, a dry purr. "I'm sure he did." She looks at the assembled jakes, her voice pitched to carry. "Well. This is a puzzle."

This time, it's the jakes who laugh. My stomach twists; Gem doesn't understand, and I dread the point where I'll have to explain it to him. Or maybe I'll be spared the task. Savu spies his confusion, a slow smile spreading across her face.

"You see, dear Gem, your Snow is princely here. Inviolate. Any who harm him break the peace. And harmed him you have, by bringing your enemies here."

I step forward without volition. "Savu, please. He didn't do this—"

"And yet he caused it to happen." Her words are iron. She looks at Gem, assessing. "Such ignorance demands, at the least, compensation."

On cue, Nixa steps up and hands over the satchel. "He was carrying *this*," she says.

Savu looks at the lancet and coil. She blinks, reaching in to touch without revealing either object to the prying eyes of the court. "Well, now. This *is* unexpected. It will make a pretty payment."

"Please." Gem gulps the word, his hands still twined behind his back. "We've need of that, or I wouldn't have brought it. I can find other gifts—"

"Find?" says Savu, deceptively mild. "Why should I care what you can *find*, compared to keeping this?"

Gem licks his lips, desperate. "I have contacts, skills—"

"Enough."

The word rings through us like a bell. Gem cowers, breathing too hard for how little he's said, and I wonder how much of his trembling is down to fear for Reeve, and how much to his memories of this place; of the last time a junza-boss stared him down here and bid him do their will.

"You have no licence to barter with me, Gem the Diamond," Savu says. "You aimed above your always and left; don't think to come back to the junzas without cost or consequence. You're lucky I only take this, and not your blood. Be grateful. Now—"

"I'll trade you a death," I say.

The whole court stills. The whole court stares. My gaze is locked on Savu.

"A death," she repeats, with genuine surprise. "You'd trade me a death for this?"

"You know what I'm offering."

She doesn't deny it; there'd be no point. I've traded deaths with the junzas before, but never often, and only ever at their asking. The rules for such an exchange are set in stone, bound up in the peace I forged after Tamek. But Gem doesn't know that, and so stares at me, utterly horrified.

"Snow, what are you *doing*?"

"Shut *up*," I hiss back.

Gem snaps his mouth shut, then lets it fall right open again as Savu says, "Three deaths."

"Two," I counter. "One for that—" I nod at the satchel, "—and one for his trespass."

Savu considers, then nods her head. "Done."

"So witnessed," says Nixa. The words are echoed by all the Scapegrace jakes, a murmured pledge: *so witnessed*.

Savu rises from her throne. She waves for the musicians to play again, which they do; though some jakes continue to watch us all, the rest resume their chatter. With this done, she comes to stand before us: she's taller than Gem as well as me, and not just because of her wedge-heeled boots. She hands me the satchel, lips quirking as I pass it straight to Gem, who pulls it back on like a piece of dropped armour.

"Snow Kidama," she says, amused. She cups my cheek in her calloused hand, her strong thumb stroking my cheek. "You truly are what you've always been." She drops her hand before I can dare to ask if that's a compliment. "Where are you headed?"

"Argos Precinct," I say.

"Hm." She slides her gaze to Gem. "You have gatepasses?"

"I do."

"Fakes?"

"Good fakes."

She scoffs. "The shields are skittish right now. You'll be caught."

Gem bridles. "You have a better idea?"

"Much better," says Savu, ignoring his glib. She summons Nixa with a wave, and the hand comes to stand with her, listening as Savu talks. "There are tunnels beneath the Dio—old paths built when New Arcadia was still fabled Jerichae. Let Nixa accompany you on your errand, and I'll grant you their use."

It's phrased as a bargain, but I know an ultimatum when I hear one. Gem's jaw works, but as many years as he's been gone from Charybdis Precinct, he knows enough not to argue now.

"We'd be honoured," he grits out.

"As well you should be," Savu says. She turns to Nixa, smiling her first real smile of the night. "Go with them. Guide them. Keep them safe." *And report back to me*, she doesn't say; but then, she doesn't need to.

"Of course," says Nixa, smiling in turn—and then Savu leans in and kisses her, and Nixa kisses back. That none of the jakes around us seems surprised by this development tells me I've been away from the court for too long; Gem just gawks, but under the circumstances, I can hardly blame him.

They break apart moments later, still smiling. "Luck," Savu murmurs, tugging playfully on one of Nixa's white-streaked locs.

"Luck," Nixa echoes, grinning.

With that, Savu turns on her heel and reclaims her throne, stretching out like a cat in a sunbeam. Nixa looks at her fondly, then smacks me on the arm.

"Well, then," she says, full of grating cheer. "Let's go."

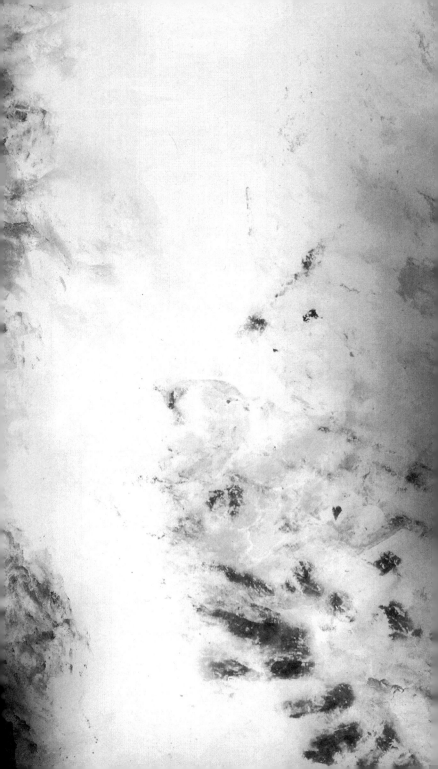

V

WE MAKE IT all of two blocks from the court before Gem, who's been storming along in silence, suddenly stops and says, "No."

"No what?" I ask, tartly. Nixa looks between us, sighs, and slouches back against the wall of a neighbouring building, tipping her gaze beseechingly skywards.

Gem forces the words through gritted teeth. "No, we are not pretending you didn't just agree to murder *two people* to get us out of there!"

Nixa chokes with laughter, but it's me who gets Gem's glare. I run a hand down my face, abruptly too tired for all of this.

"That's not what happened."

"You sure, Snow? Because that's what it fucking sounded like."

"It's part of the peace," I snap at him. "I'm partisan with the bosses, the jakes. I can't be forced to work as a vox by any of them, but I can agree to trade my skills, provided it's not to excess or skewed to favour one junza. The next two times Savu kills someone with knowledge she wants—and she does kill; all the bosses do, you surely remember that much—" Gem flinches, which I refuse to find satisfying, "—I'll be there to speak answers from their ghosts. *That's* what I traded."

Gem looks first dumbstruck, then wary, and then just a little afraid in a way that makes my guts twist.

"There was never peace in the junzas," he says, voice rough. "What the fuck did you do to make one?"

My temper sparks again. "You haven't sussed it yet?"

"I want to hear you say it."

"Fine." I step into his space and lift my chin, angry and uncowed. "After what Tamek did to us, I thought you dead, and I let him think me broken. I played at being his pet vox, but Sohlan went to Rilke and Savu and treated with them on my account. We reached a deal. I killed Tamek myself, while he slept. I gave his court to Savu, split his junza between her and Rilke. We built the peace on that; we built the peace on *me*. I speak for the dead of this precinct. I take no sides. That's what I do, now. That's what you're paying me for."

"And you never left," Gem says, softly. "Even with Tamek dead, you stayed."

A shudder runs through me, strong as a shockjack's current. "Of course I stayed," I say, voice thick, and now I can't look at him. "You were *dead*, Gem. I had nothing else."

Gem has no answer to that. We look at each other: too close, too soft. The night air presses in like a cool, dark cloth.

"We should go," murmurs Nixa, breaking the silence. "Come on."

She starts walking again, not waiting for us to follow. For once I'm glad of the interruption: it forces me to rip myself away from Gem; from how it feels to have him look at me like that.

We move through the precinct like ghosts, and do not speak.

❦

AT THE NORTHWEST edge of Savu's junza, Nixa leads us into a guarded storehouse—one of the court's supply caches—and down to a gloomy basement where iron troughs of soil and pungent shit grow row upon row of mushrooms. The old rhyme comes to my head, unbidden: *white to eat and blue to glow, red to kill and grey to know.* All common types are represented here, along with some others: a Charybdian fortune in poison, food and hallucinogens, with just enough bluecaps sprinkled in for visitors to see by. Their skinny, luminous crowns stand proud of their shorter fellows, like the eyestalks of deep-river creatures.

Navigating through the rows, Nixa leads us over to the far wall, where she promptly orders Gem to prise up an anonymous paving slab. He complies with a grunt, unleashing a gust of silty air. An incongruously rust-free ladder leads the way down into darkness. At Nixa's urging, I descend first, hands clammy on the cold, clean metal. Forty rungs down, my feet hit stone. With no light to see by, I gingerly feel my way to the wall and wait, listening to the juddering scrape as the paving slab is tugged back into place, the echoing scuffs of Nixa and Gem's descent.

"Here," mutters Nixa. There's a rummaging sound, followed by a soft click and a sudden wash of soft, white light. I blink the stars from my eyes to find her holding a levitan torch: a wand of glass powered by a lightning-infused crystal set in a leather-wrapped grip. Though all six gifts can imprint on lyracite, only a levitan's power can move through other materials without its aid. The torch is one such use; my shockjack is another.

Now that we can see, the tunnel is revealed to be made of dark brown stone, the floor worn smooth by the passage of boots and time and sloping faintly downwards. The walls are damp, uneven and patched with moss, spaced just widely enough for two people to walk abreast. Nixa takes the lead with her torch, leaving Gem and me to follow. The ceiling slopes downward; I wonder how long it'll be before we're beneath the river.

"I never knew this was here," Gem murmurs. His voice echoes strangely, as does Nixa's answering laugh.

"They'd hardly be secret if you did."

We walk on in silence. The sloping ground gives the feeling that we're strolling down a throat. I sneak glances at Gem, at his profile in the torchlight. *Who is Reeve to you?* I want to ask. It's a greedy, useless question to which I'm not owed an answer; it gnaws at me anyway.

"So," says Nixa, once more my unwitting saviour. "You two going to let me in on whatever scheme you're running as needs a brand new vox's kit, or am I meant to jump in blind?"

Gem makes a face. "I suppose we don't have a choice," he says, more resigned than ungrateful, and gives her the same bare-bones he's given me.

Nixa stays quiet through the recitation, and for a good few seconds after. Then, in an overly careful voice, she says, "You're really working with the Red Steps?"

"Yes."

"And trying to break into the lyracite mines to prove the Stonemetal Guild corrupt?"

"Yes."

"Which will piss off each and every goldplate quartz-dealer with stakes in this city?"

"Yes."

"You're a fucking lackwit," says Nixa. "Yuhiqa's bloody clutch, I must've heard worse plans before, but I sure as fuck can't think of 'em right now."

"You don't have to come," I tell her, just to be petty. "You could always say we slipped you and run back to Savu."

Nixa snaps her free hand back and smacks me semi-affectionately across the head, which is both answer and fair turnabout. With a long-suffering sigh, she says, "All right, then. Tell me more about this Reeve fel we're foxing. He from Argos?"

I tense a little in anticipation. Gem hesitates. "No, not from Argos?"

Nixa shoots him an exasperated look. "Where, then?"

Too quickly, Gem says, "From Rubicon. But—"

"From *Rubicon?*" Nixa exclaims. She comes to a dead halt, whirling on her heel and slapping Gem's head far harder than she did mine. "You utter *mawk*! You're risking all this for a fucking *goldplate*? Kithani's tits, if you're getting up and under with him—"

"No!" says Gem, hotly. "No, we're not—it's not like that, not either part of it. His family disowned him years ago, and he's not…he's got no interest in men." And I'd take some comfort in that, if not for how he falters when he says it.

Nixa groans for the both of us. "Oh, *that's* better. You ain't even fucking him, you just wish you was!"

"So what if I've thought about it?" Gem shoots back. His accent slips out when he's angry, making him sound betrayingly like the Gem I remember. "That's not why I'm doing this! Reeve risked his life for us, for a better city, and if that's what it's cost him, then I owe him to finish this right." And then, bitterly, "Of all people, I know what it means to start over from nothing."

Nixa snorts, but doesn't probe him further. An ugly part of me hates her for that, craving a stoush for which I've got no stomach. I say nothing, but though Gem has no alethian's gift, he reads my thoughts clear in my face.

"Go on, then," he snaps. "Chew me out for lusting over a fallen goldplate! I'm sure it matters more than what's going on in Argos."

I take the bait like some zamfool fish in the Dio. "What's
to chew? You've fucked worse, me incl–"

"*What's* going on in Argos?" Nixa asks sharply. "Savu
said the shields are out, but not even she knows why."

"Maybe she does, and she just hasn't told you," I mutter,
stung.

Sensibly, Nixa ignores my pique and focuses on Gem.
"Well?"

Gem slumps, running a hand down his face. "Trouble,"
he says. "Unrest with the miners. If they're not already
rioting, it won't be long. There's a reason we've been
looking into the Stonemetal Guild now, of all times;
there's a reason why this matters."

He cuts his gaze to me as he says this last, and I try to
make myself concede the point, to put my hurt aside.

There's a moment of silence, and it takes a beat too
long for me to realise Nixa and Gem both think I'll
speak. Stuttertongued, I falter at the threshold of their
expectations. Our footsteps echo loudly in the tunnel,
and for the first time I hear the drip of water, distant and
unnerving. How much of the river lies above us? How
strong must this stonework be to bear its weight?

Nixa comes to my rescue. "What's the spark?"

"Cinch any belt too tight, the buckle bursts," says Gem.
"It's not one thing, but one thing after another. There's more
and more quartz in Argos, more and more salaried miners
either being pinched out for prisoners or found with quartz
and called addict, criminal—sometimes truthfully, sometimes
not." His expression darkens. "Of course, they still *need* skilled
workers; it's just that the Guild and the goldplates don't care
to pay them, so the ones that remain are overburdened and
underpaid and terrified they'll be framed as users if they
complain, and meanwhile all of Deyos wants more lyracite."

"And you really think," I say, "that this—this
Assemblyman Vitho—" I rifle my thoughts to recall his
name, and find it tastes bitter in my mouth, "—will truly

act on proof of Guild corruption? You truly think that,
even *if* he acts, it will actually matter?"

Gem is silent for half a breath too long. "I do," he says.
Then amends, more truthfully: "Or at least, I hope so.
The only other path to change is raw violence, Snow, and
New Arcadia sees enough blood as it is."

"We live in a city of walls," I say, and slap my palm on
the tunnelside for emphasis. The impact makes a soft, dull
thump, and in the light of Nixa's torch, I see there's still
blood on my quartz-grey fingers.

Gem's blood, still barely dry.

Shuddering, I wipe them clean on a patch of moss and
add, a bit too hurriedly, "You said it yourself: so long as a
problem stays within its precinct, nothing changes. The
junzas run Charybdis, the Guild rules Argos, the goldplates
sit in Rubicon and Midas, the scholars crouch in Daedalus
and the Kithans keep Virgil and Juno. Jerichae's walls
belong to New Arcadia now. The city is what it is."

"Nothing lasts forever," Gem counters. "There's places
outside the city, Snow, and they care what happens here."

I laugh, the sound barbed in my throat. "They care
because we have lyracite."

Gem makes a frustrated sound. "That's not all we have,
and we're not even the only ones who have it. There's
other mines in Cadence, Thyris, Salome—"

"And do they help us?" I don't mean to shout, but the
cold stone throws my voice back at me, loud as a slap.
I halt and grab Gem's arm so that he stops, too, then
drop him like a hot coal. Nixa swears softly, but doesn't
intervene; she's used to the tempers of jakes, and what else
are Gem and I to each other but that?

I swallow around a swollen tongue, my mouth gone
paper-dry. "You come back here," I say to Gem, "and
tell me about these lofty places you've never seen—that
I'll never see—and lecture me on what change is, but
you know *nothing* of what I've done without you here;

what I've had to do to keep the Dark Heart beating
steady. Nothing!"

I see him flinch, and some terrible part of me roars
in satisfaction. I step in close to him, staring up at those
wide, dark eyes agleam with Nixa's light. Soft and deadly,
the words pour forth. "You left me bloody and broken on
the floor of Tamek's court, Gem the Diamond, and even
so, I mourned you. It was Sohlan who mended me—
Sohlan alone, not you, because *you weren't there*. You stand
there and judge me for selling deaths to Savu and Rilke,
but how much fouler would the junzas be, if I hadn't
mortared that truce in blood? I am *full up* with ghosts,"
I spit, or maybe croak, "and now you come here—you
come back from the fucking *dead*, Gem, and you ask for
help with some new cause in place of the one I thought
killed you?" I shove him hard in the chest, tears hot in my
eyes. "*Fuck* you!"

Gem just stares at me, silent and shocked. I smack my
fist into his chest, but he doesn't move, just looks at me like
I'm something he doesn't understand and can hardly bear
to witness. How alien must I be to him—to Nixa, to every
haunted soul in Charybdis who begs me speak to ghosts?
I burn and tremble and scream without screaming, my
throat squeezing every breath thin and wild, until I'm
choking on all the air I suddenly don't know how to
breathe; and amidst all this invisible chaos—as Gem just
looks, and looks, and *looks*—it's Nixa who saves me, Nixa
who puts her wiry arms around my bones and hugs me
back against her chest, her voice a soothing patter as I go
to my knees and she kindly follows.

"Snow, Snow, shh, come now, come now. Come back,
chuska'ti, you're good, you're here. Snow, hey, Snow—just
breathe—" and then she slips into Deyosi, soothing as
warm milk, though I barely speak it, "—tiavo taq, aya
dana re'vi, na? Come on, come, shh, hey—there you are.
There you are."

I slump in her arms, cold salt on my cheeks and colder shame in the place my rage has fled. I try so hard not to be like this, but it catches me every so often, and after the day I've had…it's all been too much to stay swallowed down, and now I have to be witnessed at my worst.

"I'm sorry," I rasp, and tell myself the apology is for Nixa alone, not Gem. "I'm not myself."

"It's all right," says Nixa. I've never known her gentle like this, her voice as calm as I once imagined my mother's would be, and part of me wants to weep all over again, that I've forgotten the softness of jakes towards their own. I stifle the impulse and straighten; Nixa pats me on the shoulder, and when we come to our feet again, it's as if I never faltered.

Gem looks at me. Swallows. Looks away.

We walk on in silence.

VI

W E LEAVE THE tunnel in much the same way we entered it: up a ladder, through a trapdoor and into a dingy basement, though this one is free of mushrooms. Nixa squints and shines her torch in the darkness, revealing a pile of dusty crates, a table and stools, and a short flight of stairs to a closed door set high in the wall.

"Well, this ain't good," she mutters. "This place is meant to be guarded."

"Maybe they're upstairs," says Gem.

Nixa says nothing, but switches the torch to her off-hand, resting her right palm on the hilt of her knife. Soft-footed, she leads us up the stairs, and damned if Gem and I don't fall into our old flanking spots behind her—him on the right side, me on the left, the way we used to pair off in the Bonebreak crew. I ride out my shudder and watch as Nixa knocks a quiet pattern on the heavy wood, announcing us.

Nothing happens.

Nixa swears softly. Knocks again, louder this time, but still nothing happens. She chews her lip, hesitates, then reaches into her shirt for a hidden key strung on a loop of braided leather. As she unlocks the door and eases it open, my fingers itch for my shockjack.

Nixa stares into the upstairs room for a long, quiet moment. Then she turns and beckons me up, her face blank. She steps back enough for me to walk past her, holding the door open.

"Tell me what you see in there, Snow."

I ought to be prepared for what I find, but I'm not. Of course I'm not.

"This fucking day," I curse, and cross the threshold.

The dead woman lies facedown, her matted hair white and her skin mottled grey, its oily sheen limned blue by a trio of bluecap globes. The room stinks of death and mushrooms, but I'm used to that; I block it out and fix my gaze on her flickering umbra, which kneels nearby, staring blankly at nothing.

"I see you," I say.

The ghost turns to look at me, slow and sad.

"I took too much," it says, a note of puzzled helplessness in that soft, unreal voice. "Everything hurt, so I thought I'd try the white, just a little white, but I needed more and more again, and then I took too much."

Behind me, I hear Gem's shocked inhale—he can't hear the ghost, but he's surely seen the body. I focus on the umbra, which shows me a woman around my own age, brown-skinned and brown-haired, dressed in worn but functional leathers. She must've been truly new to quartz, for her umbra to show no echoes of her addiction: it means she still thought of herself as she was before. The quartz must've taken her hard and fast—too much of a mean, cruel batch.

"What's your name?" I ask.

The umbra shivers. "Damri," it sighs—and then dissolves, as quick as snapped fingers.

I breathe and turn,meet Nixa's gaze, ignore Gem's. "Her name was Damri," I say. "She died of an overdose."

Nixa blanches. "*That's* Damri?" she breathes. "Manaan's *arse*."

I let out a heavy breath. "She's Scapegrace, then?"

"No, but near as good as. We trusted her here, to parlay with the Argos mobs. I saw her, what—two weeks ago? Three? She didn't look like this. Not a lick of pale on her then, that I could see."

"Argos quartz is strong of late," Gem murmurs. "Too strong for many, but still too weak for some. No doubt it'll be in Charybdis soon, too."

Nixa looks like she wants to spit, but remembers the corpse and thinks better of it. Instead, she stoops and pats down Damri's pockets, pulling out something she hides in her own too quickly for me to see.

"Ushai bring you peace," she murmurs, pity in her tone. Straightening, she adds, "We'll have to leave her for now." She flashes a look at me, half apology and half query as to whether a sorry is needful; I shake my head in answer. Relieved, she nods and picks her way forward, holstering the levitan torch. The room is small: a caretaker's space hidden in some larger building, likely another warehouse. A cot is set against one wall in an alcove sized for the purpose; another, smaller, curtained area hides a latrine and a nightsoil box, the contents borrowed to feed the mushrooms.

Damri lived and died here, safe from everything except herself.

Reaching the far wall, Nixa runs her hands over the panelling until something clicks. With a muted *shhh*, a section of wood pops out and slides aside, revealing an entrance to the building beyond. We slip through quickly, then wait for the door to shut itself, invisible unless you know what to look for—like many such failsafes, the mechanism allows it to open for only a brief period.

There's no lock on Damri's side, but a key is likely needed
to open it from where we are now; which is, I realise
belatedly, most likely what Nixa took from the body.

"Careful, now," she murmurs. "This should be safe, but…"

But Damri's dead, so who knows what else has changed? No
need to state the obvious. I peer around us, blinking in
the gloom. We're in a cramped and crowded warehouse
stacked to the rafters with boxes, crates, miscellaneous
objects—a supply cache for the Scapegrace junza.
Everything's jammed in tight enough to make the place a
maze, which is likely deliberate, the whole room lit stingily
by a single ancient levitan-bulb strung from the central
ceiling, as yellow and dim as a drunkard's eye.

"Jakes up front?" I ask Nixa—meaning, are there more
Scapegrace stoushers guarding the cache outside?

Nixa frowns, lip curled like a cat's. "Oughta be," she
mutters, "but this place don't take priority if there's bigger
mischief, and—"

She stops again as we turn a corner, words and walking
both. Gem and I copy, tracking her frozen line of sight to
a single grimed and iron-barred window set high in the
wall. Light flickers behind it, red-brown and incongruous.

Firelight, in a place no fire should be.

"Yuhiqa's bloody clutch," snarls Nixa, glaring at Gem.
"What hive did your Steps kick over? Don't answer that,"
she adds, when Gem opens his mouth. "This *fucking* city.
Gods, but I hate fire!"

We reach the front door, which is latched from the
inside, and wait again as Nixa knocks against it in a
pattern. This time, though, there's no surprise when no
one answers, and after four seconds, Nixa unlocks the
door and lets us through.

Smoky air hits us—smoke, but no heat, which is as
good a sign as we can hope for. The upper floor of the
neighbouring warehouse is on fire, flames licking through
the rafters, but a human chain hauling buckets of sand

is already formed in the alley opposite, working folk shouting and organising to put out the blaze. Quickly, Nixa pulls out a key—no, two keys on a single clip, the ones she took from Damri—and relocks the warehouse behind us.

"Come on," she murmurs, turning away from the burning building. She pauses before setting off, untying the green band that marks her as a Scapegrace jake and stashing it in a pocket. "Mining district's this way."

Lamps and firelight cast the broad, smooth streets and dirty, narrow alleys in flickering gloom as Nixa leads us onwards. By night or day, I've never seen Argos Precinct before, but I'd guess the warehouse district doesn't usually churn like a kicked-over anthill this long after sunset. Spot fires are everywhere, and so too are fire crews armed with smothering sand, Argosi protecting their own as keenly as Charybdi do.

"They're lucky none of it's spreading," says Gem, as we pass by a bigger blaze.

I snort. "It's no luck at all. Look at them! Dozens of tiny fires high up, burning apart in patterns that have nothing to do with the wind? They're not meant to spread. Whoever set them did it as a distraction, to draw all this attention away from somewhere else."

Nixa nods, but Gem looks slapped. "The Red Steps wouldn't do that," he says, a bite of defensiveness to the words.

"I never said they would," I snap, though of course it's a possibility.

"Probably the shields or the Stonemetal Guild," says Nixa. "They want an excuse to raid around while folks are busy, slap blame on anyone who's been causing them grief elsewhere."

"Or else hide one particular crime amidst others," I add. "Like those murders last year."

"Murders?" asks Gem.

Nixa makes a disgusted noise. "Some zamfool jake from Bloodthread got ambitious. Decided to off one of his boss's men to take his place, but tried to hide it by making the kill distinctive and doing the same to—how many poor civs was it, Snow?"

"Three," I say. "Would've been four, but the last one got away."

"Pathetic. Jakes like that're less use than a duke in a dovecote." She flashes me a grin. "Present company excluded, of course."

It's an old tease, worn almost comfortable with use. A duke like me might have no interest in women, but I've spoken more than one ghost in Charybdis's female-staffed brothels, to say nothing of the mixed and male-staffed kind. I roll my eyes at Nixa and she grins back in the darkness, unrepentant.

We fall silent as another fire crew runs past us, pressing ourselves to the shadows of an alley. My pulse spikes, remembering the ambush back in Charybdis scant hours ago, the terror of nearly losing Gem again. I watch him in the half-dark, eyes fixed ahead as he scans Nixa's route. The urge to touch him, to prove he's real, is so sudden and sharp it's like being stabbed. I choke on a breath too big for me, and somehow follow as we move again, criss-crossing a series of curving streets until we're skirting an open plaza. It looks like a market-space, but at the side nearest to us is a square pit, the edges tiered into three deep steps leading down to the bottom. Light glints off drains in the floor, and the purpose clicks: it's a fighting pit.

Jagged memories strobe my thoughts like a shockjack's lightning. Savu's court has such a pit that once was Tamek's: more crude by far than this clean Argosi cousin, yet no less viciously used. Gem left me a bloody wreck in that pit, and Tamek left each of us in turn to think the other dead. Eight years have passed, but the belt of numb

flesh around my waist where Gem broke my back is mine
forever, the nerves severed beyond even Sohlan's ability to
fix them. Eight years, and dreams of that fight still have
me waking hollow and sweat-soaked: the shouting jakes,
the terror and rage of the boys we were, and everywhere
Tamek, roaring laughter as he made us fight or die.

I look away, mouth hot with remembered salt, blood,
tears. I've never blamed Gem. Has he blamed me?
There's been no space to talk of it, and who's to say there
ever will be, once we find his Reeve?

"Wait," says Gem, as Nixa makes to choose a new
turning. "Reeve's contact is this way. Wheel Street, nearer
the wall."

Nixa inclines her head. "After you," she says, and lets
him take the lead.

I make no comment, and follow.

※

REEVE'S CONTACT—AND by extension, Gem's—is a hard-
eyed miner in her late forties, thick all over with muscle,
arms ropy with scars. Her name is Rin, and her house on
Wheel Street is sparsely furnished, neat except for the dust
she tracks in from the tunnels. If anyone lives here with
her, they're either absent or hiding, but a tortoiseshell cat
sleeps curled on a chair in the corner, and something in
me settles at the sight of it. I've known plenty of rotten-
souled folks to keep dogs or other beasts they can train
to anger, but where scrape is scarce and food scarcer, it
speaks to kindness to keep an animal that can't protect
you or earn you coin. Doesn't mean Rin can't be her own
shade of cutting or cruel where needed, but at least I know
she's got some softness to her.

Not that it's visible now, as Gem tells her the shape of
our plan: that we're hunting Reeve and need her help to
retrace his path into the lyracite mines.

"You've picked a hell of a time to come asking favours," Rin says. She crosses her arms and glares at him like he's three coins short of a levy. "Did you walk here with your eyes closed?"

"We saw the fires," Gem says.

Rin scowls. "You're lucky you didn't see shields. There was a protest near-turned riot at sundown out at the Guildhall, good folks asking for better treatment. It all dispersed when the Kithans got involved, cooled down the few real hotheads—some of your Steps among them, Gem," she adds, and he winces in apology. "Yet hours later, the warehouse district is burning. Everyone with sense knows the shields set the blazes, but any merchants with an eye to sympathy will suffer burned goods and be told it was the fault of the same miners who're out there right now with sandbuckets trying to save them. Meanwhile there's unbadged shields about, trying to plant quartz in our houses so's they've got an excuse to chain us when they come knocking tomorrow, citing *public safety*."

"Fucking shields," says Nixa. Everyone nods, which mollifies Rin somewhat; at least she knows we understand.

"Even so," Gem says, after an awkward beat. "That's why we need to find Reeve. If he can prove the corruption—"

"You think the goldplates give a shit?" Rin snaps. "Corruption is what keeps them rich. Always has done, always will do. Nothing you find will change that."

"Then why'd you help Reeve get in?" Gem counters.

"Because Reeve had the sense not to ask for help in the middle of a godsdamn *crisis*! What do I care what he did? He's not my kin, and at least *he* offered me payment."

Gem falters at that, but I understand Rin's anger; I've felt it often enough. "If that were true," I say, level as I can manage, "you wouldn't care that the Red Steps were sparking riot, or that the shields are planting quartz. If you really believed there's nothing to be done with the way things are, you'd either be out there lighting fires or shrugging at them, not calling them crisis."

Rin looks ready to hit me. "What the fuck do you know of it, quartzborn?"

I smile, mouth twisting crookedly. "I know that the only way out is through. I don't believe in the gods, but whether Vaia rules it or not, change is still the most powerful force in the spheres, and the most eternal. Look at where we are!" I fling out an arm to indicate the whole of New Arcadia. "You think the folks who built Jerichae's walls intended our inheritance of them? You think whoever held this land before that intended Jerichae? Some evils never go away, but it's better to let them starve than feast. Maybe the Assembly won't listen or care, but if they don't, that doesn't mean no one else will, or that trying was always pointless. There's too much grief in the world already."

I stop, heart racing more than the speech deserves, and flush to realise I'm being stared at: by Rin, by Nixa, and by Gem, whose gaze rakes sparks along my skin. Only the cat ignores me.

"And what will you do if Reeve's already dead, hm?" says Rin, after two full seconds have passed. "What if I take this risk for nothing?"

"I'm a vox. Alive or dead, I'll have his testimony."

Rin rocks on her heels, considering. Nixa watches her, but Gem still watches me, and I wish that he'd stop except for how I don't. I twitch with the urge to return his stare, but the moment is too fragile for that, and when Rin huffs, it breaks.

"All right," she says, and grins at last, for all that she looks exhausted with the lot of us. "I'll get you in, but if you get caught, you're on your own."

"Of course," says Gem. They shake on it.

We head back into the night.

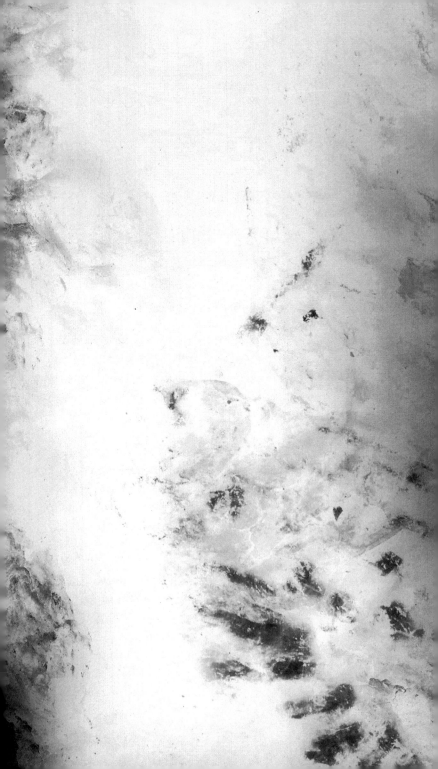

⚜ VII ⚜

"A LL RIGHT," SAYS Rin, voice pitched low as she leads us through the twists and turns of the mining district. "Whatever you know, or think you know about the mines, I'm going to assume you really don't, so you shut up and listen, just so's *I* know you've been told what's needful." She pauses at an intersection, gesturing silence as her sharp eyes scan the streets. There's as few lamps lit in this part of Argos Precinct as in Charybdis, but she won't let Nixa draw her levitan torch. Three heartbeats later, I understand why: two figures flit beneath the sputtering glow of a lonely lamp, the gleam on their armour marking them as shields. Gem swears softly, and when Rin finally steers us on, she doesn't speak again until we're two streets past their turning.

"The first thing you need to know," she says, as though there's been no interruption, "is that it's not only lyracite being mined out there. It always shows up with other stones and metals, never alone. In our mines, that means mostly silver and quartz—the crystal, not the drug," she adds, sensing my startlement, "—but also copper and electrum; sometimes even raw gold, too. Which means some tunnels are watched more close than others." She lists the names and numbers of the major shafts, and what we can expect from each, all while navigating the streets.

"Second thing," she says, "is that the prison-crews mostly get put on the higher-value shafts. Partly that's to piss on us as work for a wage—we get paid extra the more valuable metals we bring in, so the Guild saves coin if we're only finding copper and quartz—but it's also so's they don't have to stretch the guards too thin. Put all the risk in one place, right? And the prison crews are housed up top on the Spill—" the name of the hills above the mines, though it takes me a moment to place it, "—which is where the smelter is, so it's harder for them and us to mingle. But what that means is, those shafts should be mostly empty until the dawn shifts start. You'd have a hard time breaking into anything topside, but I doubt Reeve's there; if he's alive, they'll be keeping him in the foreman's round, and if he's dead, well." She flicks a meaningful glance at me. "You'll still want the lyracite tunnels."

Gem doesn't openly acknowledge her bluntness, but even in the dark—even after a decade apart—I still see how he tenses at it. "What's the foreman's round?"

"I'm coming to that," says Rin, then halts sharply, gesturing for us to flatten against the wall as shouts and running footsteps echo through the streets ahead. It's not shields this time, but a quartet of young Argosi, angry and armed. Whatever their destination, they're clearly trying to get there quickly, and they pass us by without incident. Rin's brow furrows as she watches them go, but when she speaks again, her tone doesn't change.

"The foreman's round is the mine's upper level, a big ring floor around a central well. There's a cage-lift there that runs all the way down to the deep tunnels, a winch for hauling loads up top, and a smatter of rooms—caves really, but most have doors or bars—carved into the rock. There's the infirmary, storage space, that sort of thing, but there's also a lockup. If your Reeve was captured instead of killed, that's where he'll be." She pauses, considering. "Unless they just 'scripted him straight to the prison crews. Then you're fucked."

"Thanks," says Gem, deadpan.

"Fascinating," Nixa adds, impatience shading her voice, "but how the fuck do we get *in*? We're nowhere near the wall."

"Don't need to be," Rin answers, sounding smug. She rounds a corner and motions us to stop again, cocking her head to indicate our destination: the Stonemetal Guild Archives. "There's your entry."

Nixa blinks, nonplussed. "To the mines?"

"To the mines."

"How?"

"There's a lift inside that leads to a tunnel," says Rin. "Goes right under the wall. The Guild heads had it made, oh, fifty years back, the same time they built the new Archives. See, any product they bring through the gates is registered and taxed by the Assembly, but the Guild don't always want to pay their dues any more than the goldplates do. It's terestri-built, so you know it's safe; the temples took a cut to keep it sly, though at least they do some good with theirs. It leads right into the end of an old copper shaft." She names and numbers it, fitting it to her earlier list. Gem nods, memorising, but Nixa's face is curiously blank.

Too late, I realise Rin doesn't know that Nixa is a Scapegrace jake. Gem never said more than that she was a friend: a necessary baldface under the circumstances, but Rin would never have told us about the tunnel if she'd known the truth, which Gem must've known in turn. That sort of ken trades more highly even than lyracite in the junzas, and here we've gone and tipped it straight into Savu's open palm.

"I get you to the lift, you do the rest," Rin says, oblivious. "You can come back out the same way, but be smart about it, or you'll have the Guild foxing you quick as quick. Or you can try and sneak out with one of the dayshifts, but that's a different sort of risky. The Guild don't always headcount on shift-end, and the maingate guards don't always check passes when we come back to the city, but sometimes they do, and if you're caught, you're fucked."

"We'll be careful," says Gem. "It's not like we have a choice."

Rin rolls her eyes as if to say she expected as much, and gives us a final set of instructions. There's a rear entrance to the Archives, but it's locked from the inside. We're to sneak around back and wait there for her to get in through the front, past the guards—as a senior mining representative, she's got official Archive clearance—and then she'll take us down to the basement and the lift. She's got no clearance for that, of course, isn't even meant to know it's there, but a stolen key works just as well.

And then we'll be in the mines.

With everything agreed, Rin strides off ahead, shoulders straight as a level. We wait until she's at the front steps, then start to move out in turn.

"You sure you want to bother with all this?" Nixa says to Gem, slyly. "You could tell your Assemblyman Whoever about this tunnel and prove Guild corruption that way. Save us a passel of risk."

"What," Gem says lightly, "and leave you with nothing to take back to Savu?"

Nixa looks briefly stunned, then chuckles. "Truly-shot, Gem the Diamond."

"Anyway," Gem says, a beat later, "the tunnel alone proves nothing. The Guild can call it an emergency exit, or say it was there when they bought the building. Exposing it wouldn't change anything, and Rin's folk

would lose an asset." He shakes his head. "Who knew
there were so many hidden paths in New Arcadia?"

Nixa snorts. "Show me a city of walls, and I'll show you
a city of tunnels. You don't put a path where it's needful,
it'll get made all the same, as sure as folks build bridges
over rivers."

"True words," says Gem, then quiets as we reach
the Archive door. I shiver, and not from the cold: we're
exposed out here, and the feeling walks chillbumps down
my neck like spider-tracks. I remember the stoushers
back in Charybdis, Gem's grunt as the blade went in, but
nobody comes for us—no shouting, no knives from the
shadows. I jump when the door clicks open, but it's only
Rin, just as promised.

"Quickly now," she murmurs, ushering us in.

It's cramped and dark in this part of the Archives,
full of shelves stacked high with dusty ledgers, maps and
paper of all sorts—decades worth of Guild transactions,
contracts, purchases, surveys. Rin moves swift and sure
through the aisles, leading us to a closed stairwell cut
into the stone foundations of the Archive, curling down
underground. Given that there's two upper floors above
ground level, you'd think the basement would be only
one flight down, but the cold steps go deeper than that.
We pass three landings, each with a closed wooden door,
before reaching a curtain that veils the rest of the flight
down. It's drab red-brown, heavy and hung in the semi-
dark; at first glance, it's easy to mistake for a dead end.
Rin lifts it aside without a word and leans us on again,
the stairs narrowing before turning down to terminate at
a fourth and final door. It's heavy oak banded with solid
metal; Rin puts her body between our eyes and the lock,
leaving it a mystery as to whether the key is magical or
mundane, though my money's on a mix of both. Nixa's
eyes narrow at that, but the door opens all the same, and
then we're through.

The room beyond is nothing but bare stone walls and a packed earth floor, the small space dominated by the frame and winch of a cage lift. The greasy light of an ageing, uncleaned levitan bulb gives the metal a sallow slickness.

"How much deeper is it?" Nixa murmurs, eyeing the contraption.

Rin snorts. "It's a *mine*, chuska. It ain't exactly shallow." She pauses for a moment, then adds, "Still, the city's on higher ground than where you're headed. Once you're in the tunnel, you'll be walking downhill. When you hit the first fork, you'll be in the shafts proper, and where you go from there is your own concern."

She flicks her hand at the cage, urging us to get going. Gem and I step forward in sync, wrists brushing as we reach for the grille. We both jolt, and my cheeks burn as he opens the cage, prompting Nixa to make a disgusted noise as she stomps in beside us.

"Wish us luck," I say to Rin, weakly.

"I wish you sense," she mutters, stepping back from the cage. I slide the grille shut, pulse fast as my view is striped by bars. "Pilot lever's there—" she nods her chin to the corner, where Gem has already set a hand on the controls, "—but there oughta be an external set when you touch down, and I'll thank you to send the cage back up, so's nobody finds it resting where it shouldn't be."

"Will do," says Nixa. She shoots an impatient glare at Gem. "Well?"

"Here goes," Gem murmurs.

The cage moves with a juddering, creaking crunch. Rin rises out of sight as the lift sinks down, faster than I'd expected; it's nowhere near freefall, but the speed still makes my stomach swoop like I'm standing over an open drop with a headwind nudging me forwards. Darkness falls as the room and its single levitan bulb slip out of view. I'm not scared of the dark, but this weird descent through stone and stale air feels like being swallowed. I tense up, ready to ask for Nixa's torch, when a second, smaller bulb hung from the cage roof stutters into life. All of us let out a sigh of relief, and still the cage goes down, down, down, the mechanism grinding away like an ore-toothed giant gnawing the bones of the earth.

Nixa kicks the cage, unable to hide her uneasiness. "Yuhiqa's bloody clutch, she might've said how long the drop takes." She pulls a face, mimicking Rin's voice: "*It's a mine, chuska, it ain't exactly shallow*—no shit, lady! That doesn't tell me how long I'm gonna be stuck in a box for!"

"Too long," Gem mutters.

I hide a grin as Nixa sharpens her stare on him.

Minutes pass, though whether it's two or ten, I couldn't say; perhaps it's even less than that. Every second feels like I'm stretching my foot for a ladder rung I can't quite reach, time sutured by unknowing. And then, without warning, we slap the ground like a drunkard's hand, set reeling in the echoing aftershocks.

Outside the cage is a sloping tunnel just wide enough for four adults to walk side by side, assuming none object to walking in minecart tracks. The lone rail terminates just shy of the cage, illuminated more by its single bulb than the bluecaps lining the tunnel walls. Gem shuts the grille as we disembark while Nixa hauls on the external lever, sending the cage back up. The light ascends with the lift, and for the seconds it takes our eyes to adjust to the lesser glow of the bluecaps, muted and familiar, we're plunged into darkness.

"Come on," sighs Nixa, striding ahead. "Let's get this over with."

Rather than walk on the rails, Gem and I fall into step behind Nixa. Our footsteps are muffled, everything washed in muted bioluminescence. The mushrooms grow in lines and clumps, not quite haphazard but far from uniform, with intermittent stretches of almost-dark between uneven clusters. The air is still and stale and the ground slopes down like a monster's throat, the gradient building a steady ache in my calves.

"So," says Gem suddenly, awkward as we traverse a dim-lit section. His gaze is fixed ahead, somewhere above and to the right of Nixa's shoulder. "Where do you live these days, if not the court?"

"Sohlan's old place."

"Sohlan," says Gem, exhaling the name like a prayer. "After you, when I—afterwards, you said he was the one who—?"

"Yes. He saved my life."

"Good. That's, I mean—" He glances at me. Exhales, soft and slow. Looks away again. "Good."

Nixa gives a long-suffering snort. We pass a flourishing crop of bluecaps, and as the brighter light throws shadows across the dirt, Gem asks, "How is he? Sohlan, I mean."

The question strikes between my ribs. "He's dead," I say, unable to keep the hurt from my voice. "Years back, now. His heart gave out."

"Oh," says Gem, stricken. He stumbles but doesn't quite stop, hurrying to keep pace with me as Nixa quicksteps ahead of us. "Fuck, I'm sorry. I should've known."

"Known how?"

"From before. When you didn't take me to him." He ghosts a hand over the ribs Emani healed, then says again, more softly, "I'm sorry, Snow."

Something in me cracks at that. It's not the first time he's said *Snow* and *sorry* since appearing in Lark's kitchen, but this time hurts like teeth in a wound. Grief is its own strange animal; it comes and goes as it pleases. I choke on it like swallowed bones and say, voice rough, "And you? Where've you been, Gem? When I buried Sohlan, when—any of it, eight years, and now you're here again—where have you been? No," I say, when he opens his mouth. "I don't—don't answer that. I know. You've been walls away. That's it. That's all. Walls away." Walls away, which might as well have been worlds. And then, in a rush, "How did you get out? When Tamek had you dragged you off, I thought—"

"It was Jhari," Gem says, running a hand through his hair. His deep voice shakes like a loose-latched door in a storm. "She and my ma were friends—had been, when ma was still alive."

"I remember." It comes out a whisper.

"Tamek didn't. He told her to kill me, dump the body—not like he needed proof I was gone, he hardly cared enough for that, I didn't matter, not like you did—" he gulps on the words, eyes dark as he flicks a glance at me, "—but Jhari wouldn't. She let me go, for ma's sake." A glimmer of pained hope crosses his face. "Is she still—?"

"No." *I'm sorry.*

He drops his gaze. "I suppose it was too much to hope." His mouth twists, bitter with irony, and then he speaks again. "Anyway, I ran. Got out of Charybdis with a bunch of day-laborers, found a bar in Argos and spent the next fortnight trying to drink myself to death. Would've done it, too, if I'd had enough scrape." He laughs, raw and shaky. "Ended up in the fight pits. That was better'n being dead. It hurt more, and I wanted to hurt."

My throat closes over. "Gem—"

"I ended up winning enough to get myself free again," he says, "and for a while, it was... well. Not good, but near enough. I had enough of a rep to get security jobs—bodyguard, bouncer. Hitman, a few times. Nothing I'm proud of. But what Tamek did, that never went away. Thinking I'd killed you—knowing I'd killed you, having to live with it anyway—it put a hole in me. Fighting filled it for a time, but after the pits...it was like being eaten from the inside out." He clenches his shirt in his fist, face twisted. "Like a mouth in me, chewing away at itself. So I tried the white."

This time, it's me who falters. "You used quartz?"

"I did. And it came closer to killing me than Tamek, eyeblind or the fights ever did." He waits a beat, a whole other story swallowed by silence, then says, "The Red Steps found me after that. Gave me something to live for. Or a reason to die that felt worth it, when I signed on. Still does, most days."

"Gem—"

"I don't expect you to care about any of this," he says, avoiding my gaze and attempt to talk both, "but I thought you should know. Why I'm doing this. Why it matters to me. Why I think—why I hope—that things can get better, maybe. If we fight for it, or if I do."

"I do care," I say, willing him to look at me. He doesn't, though, and my stomach lurches with the need to say something, anything, to make him know I mean it. "I care about you."

Gem snorts. "No, you don't. You care about who I was, not what I am now."

"You don't know that."

"You don't know *me*." He grabs my arm and stops us both. "You don't know me, and I don't know you. Not anymore."

I shake him off, stung. "I'm helping you, aren't I?"

"For *money*," says Gem, and that's—

I shove him, hard. "*Fuck* you!"

He blanches. "I didn't mean it like that—"

"Oh? How did you mean it?"

"I—"

"Manaan's arse, would you two stop it?" Nixa snaps, exasperated. I startle, gaze dropped guiltily as she turns, glaring at the pair of us. Shamefully, I'd almost forgotten her presence. "Talk your shit out later. We're trying to be stealthy, isn't that the plan?"

"Sorry," I mumble. Gem nods once and looks away. Nixa studies us both, then huffs, evidently satisfied.

We keep walking in silence.

☙ VII ☙

GEM USED QUARTZ.

The knowledge buzzes through me like a shockjack's charge, refusing to leave me be. I don't want to think I'm judging him—I hope I'm not—but it's not something I expected. Quartz use is…fraught, in the junzas, and with reason. The bosses deal in starbright, mellow and other, rarer drugs derived from mushrooms and chemistry, and most jakes use at some point—Gem and I both did—but quartz is different. Quartz comes from outside Charybdis Precinct—from outside New Arcadia, some say, though it's not like I've ever seen enough of the city to know if that's true. There's at least one boss who's tried to horn in on reselling it from the connexi, the quartz-runners, but that way lies death, and not just to the addicts who die when their quartz is cut with additives to make the supply stretch farther. The connexi don't like to share, not their profits and certainly not the wheres and hows of their product, and they don't give warnings. Still, that doesn't stop some zamfool jakes from trying.

But unless they're one of the would-bes trying to sell
it, most bosses don't like quartz. It's not just that it means
less coin recouped by crews who buy Charybdis drugs,
though that's a factor; it's that quartz *takes* in a way that
mellow and starbright don't. A skyed jake is a useless jake,
and a useless jake has no place in a junza—and how can
you hide the use of a drug that changes how you look? Up
in Midas and Juno, in Daedalus and Rubicon—hell, even
in Argos and Virgil sometimes, though I'm told that's
less common—most quartz users, once they start to show
signs of it, can pay to hide their affliction. They dye their
hair, rub tinct on their skin, and if they start to get truly
hard-up, they've kin who'll pay to help. Through Lark's
temple-gossip, I've heard of rescari in the richest districts
who make a fortune purging the blood of wealthy addicts,
keeping it so they can use and use without sinking to the
same needy depths as the rest of us. In other precincts,
there's hospices and temple healing, sanitoriums and
drying-out cures—but not in Charybdis.

Charybdis is where quartz addicts end up when there's
no one left to help. It's where you fall to, and once you've
fallen, it's rare as Ushai's mercy that you rise again.
There's quartzborn like me in other parts of the city, Lark
says, but there, it's something your family tries to hide
from the moment you come squalling out silvered with
secondhand shame. But in Charybdis, what's the point?

I fist my hands to keep myself from staring at Gem, from
picturing him with ash-white hair and skin mottled oily
silver. Just the thought of it twists me up like wire, and in the
long gloom of the tunnel, there's no hiding from why: for all
quartz scares me, some aching part of me wants to know
what it's like, just once; why so few who start it can ever stop.
Rumour says that quartzborn are either twice as susceptible
to quartz or twice as resistant—which would I be, if I tried
it? I never knew my mother, but perhaps I'd understand her
if I took the drug that stole her from me. Do I want to know?

I think back to years ago this morning, when I helped Rahina carry her son's body while the man who killed him sat skyed and insensate, unaware of anything but the bliss of quartz. What kind of person wants to know what it feels like, to feel so little? *One who has already felt too much*, a part of me whispers. *Someone like you've been since you saw your first ghost.*

I keep my eyes away from Gem and swallow the questions I have no right to ask, whose edges would only cut us both.

After almost an hour of walking downhill, the ground begins to level out. Nixa slows, using handsign to indicate the increased need for silence, and for the first time since she showed up at Emani's door, I'm truly glad of her presence. Being near Gem has rattled me, ripped me open, and I suspect he's not much better; we need Nixa here to be sensible. Gem and I move closer to her, the three of us like an arrow of jakes in the junzas.

Up ahead, the tunnel curves for the first time since we've entered it—Rin said it was terestri-built, and I've no cause to doubt it; who else could work in a line so straight?—and as we pass through a dimmer stretch of bluecap light, something near the far wall catches my eye. I grab Nixa's shirt and Gem's wrist, pulling us all to a halt, and nod my head to the distant, slumped shape of what looks like a person huddled up by the bend.

Nixa follows my line of sight and cocks her head at me, quizzical; Gem just looks nonplussed.

"You don't see that?" They shake their heads. "Ghost, then," I sigh, a little sad and a lot relieved.

Beside me, Gem goes still. "Is it Reeve?" he asks, voice taut.

"I don't know," I murmur, taking the lead as we approach. "What does he look like?"

Gem swallows hard. "Tall. Healthy. About our age. Bronze skin, but light brown hair, sort of coppery, with a wave to it. Worn about to here." He gestures shoulder-length. "Uh. Grey eyes, and usually wears an earring in his left ear, just one."

Bitterness sours my throat, and I swallow it back like eyeblind. So what if Gem wants to fuck a man who might as well be my opposite—tall and healthy, dark where I'm light and light where I'm dark, with ears un-notched enough to carry jewellery? A man who shares his cause— his hope—in a way I never could? I nod, not trusting myself to speak, and suppress the seething, ugly part of me that hopes this ghost is Reeve's.

Three paces out, the umbra lifts its head from its knees and blinks at me, long and slow. It's a man, middle-aged and haggard, skin ashy and hair white-streaked from quartz. I let out a breath.

"It's not him," I say—and then, to the ghost, "What's your name?"

Kerrec, comes the answer. *Kerrec Lore. I'm so tired. Please don't tell the guards. I just snuck down for a rest, that's all. I'm so tired.*

My heart twists, same as it always does when a ghost doesn't know it's dead. "I won't tell the guards," I say, voice soft. "Sleep all you want, Kerrec. You've earned it."

I'm so tired, Kerrec says again, and then he just… fades out, the way the light does when dusk turns into twilight, until all that remains is an afterimage that vanishes when I blink.

"Poor soul," Nixa murmurs, surprising me. It must show on my face, as she scowls and thumps my shoulder. "What? I can't have sympathy?"

"You're plenty sympathetic," I say, resisting the urge to wince and rub what will doubtless become a bruise.

"And don't you forget it," Nixa says, and leads us both on again, into the twisting bowels of the lyracite mine.

We follow Rin's instructions, silent in the earthy, blue-lit gloom. It's eerier in the mine proper: the curving shafts and uneven walls throw strange shadows everywhere, and the ground underfoot is no longer even. All of us trip more than once, though nobody is so careless as to be loud about it, even when Gem stumbles over the lifeless body of

a miner whose slack, greying face is that of Kerrec Lore. I
wince for him, wondering how long it might be until he's
found for burial, but there's nothing more to do for him,
and so we keep going, picking our way out and up.

True to Rin's word, the mine is empty at night, or the
lower levels are at least; it's once we get close to the surface
that we'll need to worry about guards. The quickest way
up to the foreman's round would be, of course, to take
the main lift in the central shaft, but that would draw
eyes we'd rather stayed fixed elsewhere, which leaves us
fumbling in the almost dark, through narrow access shafts
too newly-dug or seldom-used for natural bluecap growth,
lit only by the occasional undernourished mushroom
lantern. It makes for grim, dirty going, and yet it's cleaner
and easier still than many trips I've taken through the
junzas.

Time has no true meaning beneath the earth, and
when we finally exit onto a shallow platform abutting the
main shaft, I've no how idea how much of it has passed.
The yaw of open space is briefly dizzying: a single flight
of rough wooden stairs, secured to struts hammered into
the rock, winds up the wall to the foreman's round, with
only a flimsy handrail to protect us from the drop. There's
more and brighter mushroom lanterns hung at intervals
here—but also, up at our destination, the tell-tale glow
of at least one levitan bulb. We press ourselves to the
shadows and wait, looking up to see if any guards are
passing by, checking sightlines to where a bystander might
be waiting, but there's nothing. Nobody.

We climb.

The stairs groan beneath us like aging joints; Nixa
stifles a curse, one hand on her knife hilt as she waits to
see if the noise draws visitors, but either no one hears or
no one cares. Up we creep like hungry mice through a
pantry floor, up into light, to the smooth, naked floor of
the foreman's round. Again, we wait; again, we listen.

Nothing.

This time, it's Gem who takes the lead as we fox our way along the outer wall, one two three of us all in a row, with me betwixt and Nixa in van. We pass an empty overseer's office, storerooms, an infirmary, all locked. And then, halfway around the circumference, we hit a small, unmarked tunnel, dimly lit, that terminates in a heavy, iron-bound door. But before that, there's a handful of smaller, less menacing doors on either side, with small, barred windows set in the wood, and it's these that draw our attention.

Soft as soft, we creep closer. The first three windows show only empty rooms, dark and dusty; but the fourth is lit from within by a mushroom lantern, and Gem lets out a small cry as he grips the bars, staring desperately at what he finds.

"Reeve!" he whisper-shouts. "Oh gods, Reeve, you're alive!"

"Gem?"

The answering voice is hoarse, disbelieving. There's a clink of chain, and then Reeve appears on the other side of the bars, his grey eyes wide with shock. His unshaven face is drawn and dirty, his copper hair gleaming greasily for lack of a wash, but it doesn't tarnish the beauty of him, the strong, stark lines of cheek and jaw. I have no right to be jealous of him—it's absurd even before you consider that he's locked up and I'm not—but then, I've never been rational when it comes to Gem.

"Gem, you can't be here!" Reeve hisses, desperation stark in his face. His accent is lapsed Rubicon, the old polish still evident, but chipped around the edges. "You have to go now, before they catch you!"

"Sure we'll go," says Gem, already pulling a lockpick set from his pocket as he stoops to engage the door. "Just as soon as you're out here with us."

A sheen of sweat gleams on Reeve's grimy forehead. Wild-eyed, he cranes his head towards the big, locked door at the end of the tunnel. "They'll be back any minute! There's no time, Gem, you have to go—"

"Got it!" Gem crows as the door unlocks. He gives a little fistpump, spinning to share his grin with Nixa and me, and just for a moment, I see him as he was at sixteen, a Bonebreak jake giddy with victory.

And then he looks away again, and beams at Reeve—who smiles right back at him, full of incredulous hope—and all I taste is blood in my mouth, and the dirt of Tamek's floor.

I shove it down deep as Gem opens the cell, moving up to stand guard with Nixa as Gem goes inside. Reeve gestures helplessly at himself: there's metal cuffs on his wrists, cinched tight enough to have rubbed the skin raw, and a thick metal chain connected to a manacle around his right leg. There's a single rickety cot against the wall, barely more than a pallet, and Reeve sits down on the edge of it as Gem examines his bonds.

"We should come in, close the door," Nixa murmurs to me. "It'll draw less notice."

I nod, though my stomach rebels at the thought of being shut in here, and do as she says, wincing as the door creaks when I pull it to. Gem is muttering under his breath, letting out little clicks and hisses as he goes through his lockpicks, trying to find the right one to work on Reeve's manacle.

"You shouldn't have come," Reeve says again. His tone is a mix of despair and wonder, like he hardly knows what to do about being rescued.

"You'd have done the same for me," says Gem, oblivious in his certainty. He doesn't look up as he says it, and so misses the guilty flinch that crosses Reeve's face. It sparks something in me, angry and hot and possessive. *You wouldn't, but I would,* I think, only to cut myself on the realisation that *no, I didn't.* Gem thought Reeve gone and still came for his testimony; but in all the years I thought Gem dead, I never once looked for his ghost. I'd told myself then it was pointless—that by the time Sohlan was through healing my broken back, his umbra would've long since dissipated—but I could've still tried; could've looked for his body. Would Jhari have told me she'd let him live, if I'd thought to ask her? She'd died not long after, a random stoush over in Rilke's territory before I'd had the chance to move against Tamek, but what if we'd spoken? What if I'd known that Gem was out there, thinking me dead? Would I have been brave enough to follow him then, as I hadn't been before?

"That's one," Gem murmurs, jolting me out of my useless thoughts. Reeve's cuffs are undone, but still there's the manacle, stubbornly resisting all attempts to get it open.

"Gem, listen," Reeve says, gaze darting across me and Nixa. When Gem doesn't respond, Reeve reaches down and grabs his wrist, squeezing until he looks up. "I know how quartz is made."

Gem frowns at him, surprised. "What does that matter? What about the Stonemetal Guild making deals with the connexi?"

"Gem," says Reeve, and now his voice is desperate. "The Guild *are* the connexi—or some of them are, at least. The main ingredient in quartz? It's lyracite dust, a mining byproduct. The Guild isn't buying quartz for their workers—they're *making* it."

A foul chill runs through me, top to toe. Nixa curses, but Gem just looks frozen. He stares at Reeve for two seconds, three, then bends back down and starts working anew on the manacle.

"All the more reason to get the word out," he says gruffly, jabbing a pick in the lock.

"What's the point?" says Reeve. "Gem, *think*. However many Assemblymen are in the dark about this, there's got to be some who know—perhaps not Vitho, perhaps not many, but *enough*."

"It doesn't matter," Gem says, stubbornly. "Once people know the truth—"

"They'll what? Stop buying quartz?" Reeve laughs, the sound more than a little hysterical, and I feel a burst of cynical kinship with him. "If Vitho brings it up before the Assembly, they'll do more than just try to discredit him. They'll never let it spread as anything more than a rumour—and what can a rumour do, against the Guild? Against the Guild in *every city*, Gem, not just here—this isn't just happening in New Arcadia!" He grabs at his shoulders, wild once more. "You've got to go, you've got to get out—"

"I think," says a polished Rubicon voice, as smooth as stone and twice as cold, "that it might be too late for that."

I whirl, staring through the bars of the cell, and find myself being smirked at by a silver-haired goldplate woman, proud and healthful, flanked by a quartet of guards. She raises a delicate hand and levels a small silver gun at me—*of course she has a gun*, I think wildly, *of fucking course, nothing but the latest and best for Rubicon's finest murderers*—and sighs in mock-disappointment.

"Really, Reeve. And here you said your friends weren't coming."

"Please, no—" Reeve chokes out, and then there's a sound like a knife on zipwire as she fires at me—I'm braced for deep pain, but all I feel is a piercing sting in the side of my neck. There's a moment of shock where she fires again, hitting Nixa this time, and then I feel it: a terrible burning lethargy like an excess of eyeblind, buckling my knees as my eyes roll shut.

The last thing I see is a third dart buried in Gem's neck, and then I fall like a bag of rocks as everything goes dark.

⚜ IX ⚜

TAMEK'S LAUGHTER FILLS the world, as bloody-sour as bile. "You want to leave my service?" he rasps, his voice like sawteeth on gravel. "You want to live? Then prove it. Fight."

Across from me, a leering jake has Gem's arms pinned behind him, forcing him to kneel. I'm kneeling too, my arms trapped in a mirror of his, but it doesn't matter. Only Gem does—only the fury on his face, the terror in his eyes.

"I won't," says Gem, voice shaking. "I won't hurt Snow."

At Tamek's nod, the jake keeping Gem pinned does something to him, hard enough that his face twists in pain. I'm not so stoic; I cry out, pulling uselessly against my bonds.

"Let him go!" It comes out half a sob. "Tamek, please, it's me you want, just let him go—"

"Do not," growls Tamek, "tell me what I want." He draws his knife from its holster, wicked-sharp and gleaming. "Fight, or I'll slit your throats now and be done with it."

It's my fault that it's come to this. We were meant to sit lookout, Gem and me, waiting to fox the shattersnipe who'd snitched on

Bonebreak to Quicksharp, but my thoughts were full of what he'd murmured against my neck that morning as we lay squashed in a bed that was really too small for either of us, let alone both.

"We should leave, Snow," he'd whispered. "You'n me, together. Get out of the junzas before they eat us."

I hadn't answered then, too shocked to know what to say, and then his hands distracted me and everything was forgotten. But as we sat quiet, I'd found myself asking, "Did you mean it?"

"Of course I meant it," Gem said. "We're better'n this, Snow, and you—" he touched my cheek, his eyes so soft, "—you're a vox. Any precinct would take you, any city—"

"Stop," I said, the hope and want of it making me angry. "I can't, you know I can't."

"Why?"

"You know why."

"No, I don't." He gripped my wrist, intent. "You think Tamek's lofty enough to chase you past the walls?"

I pulled away from him. "He'd try. He'd hurt Sohlan to get me back."

"Then we bring Sohlan!"

I would've done so much for Gem, but what he was asking terrified me. "I'm quartzborn," I snapped. "You think that won't matter anywhere else? We live here for a reason!"

Gem's eyes narrowed at that, and so we argued, hissed and heartfelt, focused on each other when we should've been watching our mark.

We missed the shattersnipe, but worse than that, we missed the sound of another jake coming to check on us. He heard Gem talk about leaving, heard us raw and hurt with each other, and knew a chance to gain Tamek's favour when he saw one.

And so we're here, in the dirt of the fight-pit, told to stoush or die.

"This is all your fault!" Gem yells, stumbling as he's shoved to his feet. I see in his eyes what he's trying to do as clear as I see ghosts, and it hurts, it hurts, but there's no other path to take.

"My fault?" I shout, as I'm released in turn. "You started it, you zamfool mawk—"

"Liar!"

Around the pit, the Bonebreak jakes cheer and jeer and yell, egging us on. I let myself be angry, let everything rise to the surface like scum on the Dio, and then Gem's on me, wild-eyed and scared and furious, and I'm on him, fighting back as Bonebreak screams for blood.

How dare Gem make me hope? How dare he make me want? I take it out on him as he takes it out on me; there's blood in my eyes and in my mouth, and then Gem roars as he grapples me up—I scrabble-swing wildly, clawing his face as he drops me down, and then—

The evil crack! *is loud enough to silence even the hooting jakes. I explode in pain, white red black raw, so deep I can't breathe can't move can't think, exploding again as I hit the ground. I hear Gem screaming—not rage, not anymore, but terror, a babble of grief and fear as the jake who'd pinned him grabs him again and hauls him away from me.*

"Kill him," says Tamek, cold as death, and I want to say no, *I want to say* stop *and* wait *and* please, *but the blood in my mouth is muddying the dirt like drool; my lungs won't work, and the last thing I see is Gem, my Gem, being dragged to his death, and all I can do is shut my eyes and hope I meet him there—*

"Please," says a voice I both know and don't. "Please let them go, they mean nothing to you—"

The doubled memory chokes my mouth like swallowed cobwebs, stranding me between then and now. Is Gem alive or dead? Did I dream his resurrection? Sohlan, where's Sohlan—

"Don't presume to tell me how I feel about this," a smooth voice says, the words so like Tamek's that just for a moment, I'm twisted backwards in time again. But no, no—this is a woman's voice, an ageing goldplate with Rubicon vowels, not Tamek's harsh Charybdi rasp, and then it rushes back to me: what happened, where we are, and why. I swallow an urge to spew or swear, I'm not sure which, and keep my eyes shut, the better to feign unconsciousness. I twitch my limbs and find I'm bound to a table—I can flex my fingers and toes, even move my knees a little, but the rest of me is strapped down tight, including what feels like a leather band across my head.

That's ominous.

"I just don't understand," says the woman, exasperated, "why you insist on making things difficult. Honestly, Reeve, I understand the need for a *little* rebellion at your age—Kithan knows, I understand!—but don't you think this Red Steps business is taking it rather too literally?"

"You say that like I haven't been useful," Reeve says sullenly, and all at once, my heart kicks with the belated realisation that he knows this woman—that he is, from the tone she takes with him, most likely related to her. *Nixa was right.* Fucking *goldplates.* "I told you what I could, didn't I?"

"Begrudgingly, yes," says the woman, "but don't pretend you sought out your disreputable friends for the family's benefit. You're a *Cathan*, Reeve; that ought to mean something."

"It's why I'm still alive, isn't it?"

A forceful *crack!*, as of a cheek being slapped. "Would you prefer it otherwise, then?" the woman asks harshly. "Should I tie you down with your criminal friends, or would you rather redeem yourself?"

A beat of silence. Then: "Sorry, grandmother."

"You fucking *liar*," Gem croaks, voice raw with betrayal. My eyes snap open of their own accord, neck tensing as I strain against my straps to seek him out. He's on a table next to me, with Nixa to his right; she's still unconscious, but they're both bound as firmly as I am. Gem looks gutted, staring at Reeve like the heart's been ripped from his chest. "All this time, you were working for them?"

Reeve lowers his head and looks away, while his grandmother chuckles indulgently.

"I imagine you're the fabled Gem Sharp," she says, as though we're being introduced at a party. Her predator's smile doesn't reach her eyes, which are the same cool grey as Reeve's; Gem glares at her like he'd spit in her face if he could.

"And who're you?" he shoots back.

The woman bobs a mock-curtsey, highlighting how out of place a woman like her appears in a room like this. Her straight, silver hair is piled on her head, and she's dressed in a deep red velvet gown, high necked and short sleeved, with gauzy fabric I don't have a name for spilling out like insect wings from elbow to wrist. There's gold in her ears and at her throat, gold in the belt that cinches her waist.

"I'm Meliana Cathan, dear," she says, and by the look on Gem's face, that name means something to him that it doesn't to me. Her smile widens, pleased at the effect she's having, and glides over to a nearby bench, where she picks up Gem's satchel and pulls out the lancet and coil, regarding them with a sigh. "You know, I've heard that education is lacking in the lower wards, but really: you do realise you can't use these without a vox?"

There's a fishhook in that question, and I'm guessing Gem sees it as clear as I do, because all he does is scowl and say, "*Fuck* you."

"Such manners!" She slides the lancet and coil away, as gentle as if she were tucking a babe into bed, and turns back to us, hands folded. "Well. I suppose even rats have their uses."

"What," Gem says, trying gamely to lift his head, "you're that short on miners that the three of us will really make a difference?"

Meliana laughs. "It's sweet of you to offer, but no. There's another task to which you're far better suited. Reeve?"

I startle as Reeve steps forward from whatever he's been doing out of eyeshot, gaze downcast as he cradles a glass syringe. My heart starts to beat in my throat, a terrible fear stealing over me.

"What—" Gem starts, then stops again as Reeve approaches Nixa. "Reeve, no, please—"

Nixa jerks minutely as Reeve finds a vein in the crook of her elbow, carefully injecting the syringe's contents.

"It'll be such a tragedy for Assemblyman Vitho,"
Meliana says, sighing. "Here he is, opening his home to
reprobates like the Red Steps, and what does he get for his
troubles? Robbed and killed by a trio of quartz addicts,
who are found on the scene by my dutiful grandson—he'd
tried to stop them, you see, but arrived too late."

Reeve steps away from Nixa, moving mechanically
to swap out the used syringe with a different one from
somewhere I can't see. I knew quartz could be injected,
but the powdered form is cheaper, more common, and all
at once I'm so angry I can barely breathe.

"Don't," says Gem, and he's pleading now, staring at
Reeve with genuine fear. "Reeve, don't, I can't, I can't
take it again, I won't go back to that, I won't, do anything
else but not—"

His words choke off into a cry as the needle goes in.
I scream in wordless fury, thrashing helpless against my
bonds, but all I can do is stare at Gem as he shakes his
head, pleas petering out into incoherent mumbling as the
drug takes effect.

And then it's my turn, and I find I've room in me left
for fear.

I struggle so hard it hurts, but I might as well be a
butterfly pinned to a board for all the good it does. Reeve
taps my elbow to find the vein, and as the needle sinks in,
I realise I'm crying.

"No," I whisper, "no, no, no—"

Meliana snorts as ugly warmth floods me. "Such a
fuss!" she says. "As if you've never had it before."

I haven't, I want to say, but my tongue won't work.
There's warmth rolling through me, warmth like love that
spreads through me with every breath. I want to be angry,
I want to stay alert and fight, but quartz is stronger than
stubbornness, and it's in me now, gnawing a space for itself.

"Just let go," says Meliana, and something about her
voice drips honey. Warm voice. Warm, sweet voice.

Why was I angry? I've always been cold, and now I'm warm. There's music at the edge of things, a gentle pulsing starsong so achingly beautiful that it must be why I'm crying. My tears taste like silver. Everything floats. There's no pain in this warm, soft place. I've hurt for so long, but now I can barely remember it.

Someone's touching me, lifting me up or lifting away? It's all the same; it's all music. Voices echo in the distance. Being carried is better than floating. Arms don't hurt. Arms hold, and when I loll I see Gem there, and Nixa. Friends. My friends are here, it's warm and soft and the music spills its silver over shifting walls spangled with pulsing mushrooms, beautiful bluecaps that open like sunflowers, swell like sails. It's beautiful. Everything's beautiful, and roughwarm touch stirs a part of me I've let lie dormant for so long, so long. I want to be touched. Just touched, just held. I arch and sigh like a cat against whatever holds me up, and someone laughs in the distance, warm as thunder, and it's beautiful.

"Gem," I murmur, "Gem, my Gem," and reach for him with my lead-fingered hand, my nails opalescent as oyster shells.

"Snow," he singsongs back, "my Snow," and everything is warm.

X

RISING UP THROUGH waves of warmth, I realise someone's shaking me. I grin, though the music is fainter than before.

"Snow? Fuck, I don't even know if that's your name, just—please, you have to wake up, the others are still skyed and there's no time—"

"Hmm?" I mumble. Blinking is hard, my lids syrup-heavy and slow with sleep. There's hands on my shoulders, big and firm, and I haven't been touched like this in long enough that it makes me laugh and bare my throat, head tipping to the side as I smile at whoever it is. Which, hmm. Should I ought to know that? "Who're you?"

"Seven bless, you're with me." A burst of desperate laughter. "I'm Reeve, and I know you must hate me, but I need you to wake up, Snow, do you hear me? I need your help or we're dead."

Reeve. I know that name. I frown. I sway myself upright until a face swims into view: grey eyes, copper hair, a worried brow.

"Reeve," I say, and it comes out like taffy, long and stretched. *Reeeeeeve.* But it sparks something in me, angry and hot and unlike the steady warmth in which I've been drowsing for I don't know how long, and so I say it again and again, willing it to mean what it ought to. "Reeve. Reeve. Reeve?"

And then it comes, the sudden detail like drowning in a backwash of foetid water. I'm no longer warm; I'm hot at my core and chilled in my extremities, and I lunge at Reeve with all the strength I have in me and grab him by the throat.

"Give me one good reason why I shouldn't kill you now," I growl.

"Gem dies if you do," Reeve croaks, and I fling him away like his skin is acid, panting and hot-cold-hot as I'm suddenly made aware of a terrible ache in every muscle, every bone. "You're coming down fast, right?" says Reeve, eyeing me with terrified sympathy. "It's always like that the first time. It'll hurt like hell for an hour or so, I'm sorry, but we don't have time—"

"Time for *what?*"

"To *live,*" Reeve hisses, gesturing at our surroundings, which—

"Where are we?" I ask, a rising dread in my throat, or maybe it's just bile. Or both. I vomit without warning, a hot-sour mess that splatters over polished wood floors. I gag, wipe my mouth on the back of my hand, and stare at the artwork hung on a nearby painted wall; the cluster of levitan bulbs overhead, set in a metal mounting designed to make them look like flowers; the beautiful furniture.

"Assemblyman Vitho's house," says Reeve. "My grandmother had you brought here a half-hour back— I've been trying to wake you ever since, but Gem and that girl are still out of it."

I whirl, head dizzier than the motion merits, and almost sob to see Gem and Nixa slumped nearby. I scramble to them, cold hands fumbling at their wrists, and let out a noise when I feel two pulses, thready and slow, too slow, but there. I linger on Gem, chest hurting from more than the quartz: his eyes are shut, but there's drying tear-tracks on his cheeks.

My head an aching jumble of thought, I turn back to Reeve and fix him with the hardest glare I can manage, which isn't very. "What's going to happen? What do we need to do?"

"Vitho is due home soon." Reeve glances nervously at a nearby clock, whose ticking, once I notice it, feels like a bird-beak puncturing my ears. "When that happens, I'm meant to—kill him. And then kill you—" he flips a hand to indicate the three of us, "—and say you did it, only I was too late to stop you. And then my grandmother will show up, and everything will be used to justify harsher penalties against addicts, because if they'll do this to a man who was meant to be on their side, then what might they do to the rest of us?" His lip curls as he says it, but there's fear in his eyes.

"You're a fucking coward," I say, for the satisfaction of seeing him flinch. My head fills up with the sound of Gem's pleading, begging not to be given quartz. That sort of betrayal goes deeper than words. It's not just that Reeve lied about his allegiance; it's that he's set Gem's body against him in the worst way possible, forcing him to refight a battle he'd already won at cost. For that alone, I could strangle him where he sits.

But I don't. I don't, because I know too godsdamn well what it is to choose between death at your master's hands and the violence that master bids you do, and however much hate I have for Reeve *fucking* Cathan right now, I also need his help.

"What's the plan?" I ask him.

"We grab your friends and get the fuck out of here. I couldn't have carried all three of you, but with you awake—"

"And where do we go?" It comes out harsh, and not just because I hurt like I've been flung from a wall into icy water. "The four of us looking like this, trying to run through Rubicon? Even if it is the middle of the night, the shields would have us the second we came within sight of a gate."

Reeve blinks at me. "We're in Juno, not Rubicon."

"Didn't you say we're in the assemblyman's house?"

"We're in *one* of his houses, yes," Reeve says impatiently. "This one is in Juno. It's more private than his Rubicon residence, and—"

"All right, all right! That's better, Juno is better for us than Rubicon. But we still need somewhere to go."

"There's a Red Steps safehouse the next district over."

"I'll take it," I say. Reeve groans with relief and hurries over to help me stand. I bristle under his touch, but my legs are water and, though it shames me, I need the assistance.

Reeve waits until he's certain I can hold my own weight sufficiently to lean against the wall, then thrusts something at me: Gem's satchel, still containing the lancet and coil, along with my slightly bloodied shockjack, which someone must've removed from my ankle-sheath. I stare at him, nonplussed, and he colours faintly.

"My grandmother doesn't know I took it," he says defensively. Then: "Wait there. I need to clean up your vomit."

That makes as much sense as anything does, so I lean on the wall and close my eyes and try to summon strength enough to carry Gem's deadweight out of here. There's a faint sound of running water from what I assume is the kitchen, followed by the pad of returning footsteps. Reeve makes a disgusted noise and stoops to clean my mess. I sling the satchel on and jam my freezing hands up under my armpits, willing some of the heat from my overcooked core to warm them up, then almost double over as I'm wracked by violent shivers. My forehead is wet with sweat, my empty stomach cramping. It's been a livelong since I took either mellow or starbright, but none of those comedowns were anything like this.

For a terrible moment, I miss the dreamy warmth of the drug—a little more would see me through the worst of this, surely? But no, no—*fuck*. I curse and wish a flaming pox on Meliana Cathan and her goldplate co-conspirators.

"Done," says Reeve suddenly, jolting me out of my stupor. "Let's get them up and get out of here."

I lurch away from the wall and over to Gem—who Reeve, inexplicably, is also trying to lift. I glare at him over Gem's prone body, and after a moment he ducks his head and mutters, "Right, right."

"You take Nixa," I say, as much to ensure he knows her name as to hammer the point home, and grunt as I sling an arm around Gem. He's taller than me by a head, heavier and broader across the shoulders, but Charybdis strength is its own scrappy thing, and Mikas's body years ago this morning is far from the first deadweight I've had to lift. I stagger as Gem lists against me, struggling to get him upright: I'll carry him in my arms if I have to, but right now I'm holding out hope that he can at least keep his feet.

Somehow I get us both vertical; Gem mumble-slurs against my neck, the first sign of life I've had from him, and I'd laugh with relief if my lungs weren't burning.

"Foxfuck, you're awkward like this," I tell him, gripping his shirt for purchase.

"Ngh," says Gem.

That does make me laugh, albeit weakly. I look to Reeve, who has Nixa slung up in his arms like a murderous sack of grain, and he nods at me.

"This way. Come on!"

He leads me through the kitchen and out to the back door, swearing softly as he struggles to unlatch it without dropping Nixa. I feel a brief pang for Gem's hopes of reporting on the Guild to Assemblyman Vitho, but there'll be time for that later, assuming Reeve's grandmother doesn't decide to kill him and frame someone else in our absence.

Door finally open, I haul Gem outside and shiver anew
in the frigid dark as Reeve closes up behind us. Nixa giggles
in his arms but doesn't wake, head lolling like a doll's. The
night is made of silence and cold stars: there's no lights on
in the buildings nearby and, as we round the side of Vitho's
place, only one streetlamp lit on a distant corner. I've no
sense of Juno's layout, where we are in relation to anywhere
else, but Reeve moves with dogged certainty, leading us
away from the light and towards a shadowed alley between
two tall, darkened houses.

We're four steps in when a pair of men materialise in
front of us. We both stop dead, and I've all of a second to
feel my stomach sink through my feet when, from behind
us, I hear the distinctive, chilling sigh of Meliana Cathan's
disappointment.

"Reeve, Reeve. I'd hoped you might see reason, but
really—what sort of fool do you take me for?"

Reeve blanches and turns to face her.
"Grandmother—"

"Don't *grandmother* me, you little shit—"

"This isn't right!"

Meliana's guards are approaching, stalking toward us
slow and steady. I chance a look over my shoulder and
find a third flanking her, arms crossed over his chest. She's
still talking to Reeve who's still arguing back, and in that
moment, I know exactly what's going to happen. The
guards will get the drop on us while Reeve is gabbing.
They'll haul us back to Vitho's place to make good on
Meliana's plan, and the only reason they've not started a
stoush already is to try and keep things quiet—

I'm tired, I'm hurt, and there's nowhere to go. Adrenaline
surges through me, but the only thing in my arms is Gem.

"I'm sorry," I whisper, and as the guards step closer still,
I gather my strength and heave him at them. It's not quite a
throw, but Gem goes windmilling forwards in a way they're
not expecting, and as they react, I snatch my shockjack out

of the satchel and strike the nearest hard across the jaw. He
makes an ugly noise and falls beneath Gem, his neck at an
unnatural angle. I spin away from the second's shout; I'm
not fast enough, but I'm still so fucking dizzy that I nearly
go to my knees, and that's what saves me—his blade whistles
cleanly over my head, and before he can pull it in again I'm
rocketing up to headbutt hard beneath his jaw. The impact
feels like I've blown myself up, but I've fought through worse,
and my arm's already swinging to bring the shockjack down
on him. It caches him in the throat as he's already falling; he
makes a wet, wrenching sound and drops—

—and then something hits me from behind. Or at
least, I think that's what happens: I stagger like I've been
elbowed, and there's a dull, burning throb in the meat
of me, but there's no sharp pain, no shock. I turn and
stare, and find myself looking in puzzlement at third and
final guard, who's staring at me like a vox at his very first
umbra. He's holding a knife, and the blade drips blackish
red in the dark, and when I realise what's happened, I
burst out laughing, which only spooks him more.

He's stabbed me where I've got no feeling: right in
the belt of ever-numb flesh around my waist from where
Gem broke my back. I grin at him, Charybdis-feral, and
whip the shockjack up between his braced legs, hard. He
spasms, wets himself and falls, and I strike him over the
head for good measure, claiming his bloody knife. I'm
starting to feel a little faint, but Meliana Cathan can't
know that; not when she's glaring at me with hateful eyes,
hands trembling as I advance on her.

"You can't kill me," she says, chin pridefully high. "You
think the Red Steps won't be suspected? All you'd really
hurt is your cause."

I bark a laugh. "It's not my cause."

"Snow," says Reeve, as if he hasn't been standing there
like a useless mawk while I save our skins, "please, you
can't—"

"Can't what? Can't do to her what she would've done to me?"

"You're better than that," says Reeve, voice trembling a little. He sets Nixa down and raises his hands in a show of peace, moving to put himself between me and Meliana. "Aren't you?"

"The fuck I am," I say—just as Meliana moves like a viper, grabbing Reeve in a headlock as she pulls an elegant switchblade from a pocket I didn't know she had and holds it to his throat.

"Stay where you are or he dies," she growls, the blade digging into Reeve's jugular. She takes a step backwards, dragging her useless grandson with her. Reeve makes a shocked, croaking noise, eyes rolling like he's a spooked horse in a thunderstorm, and maybe it's just that I'm bleeding out, but I'm fucking sick of goldplates thinking nobility is something I've ever been able to afford.

"That's it," croons Meliana, taking another step back, "no need to r—"

A knifehilt blooms in her eye. I lower my arm and grin in the darkness. A thin red line appears on Reeve's neck as Meliana's grip on him spasms; he jerks away from her, face a mask of horror as he turns to see my handiwork, one palm clapped to his shallow cut. His grandmother sways for one second, two, and then she drops: first to her knees and then slumped over sideways. Her head hits the ground with a sound like an eggshell cracking.

"What," Reeve whispers, "what did you do?"

"What I had to," I say, and as her umbra winks into view, I drop my shockjack and pull out the lancet and coil.

⚡ XI ⚡

I'VE NEVER RECORDED a ghost before, but the lancet hums to life in my hands, lit up like a sunblazed mirror. I grip the coil, my magic thrumming through it like a second pulse, and as I pass it over Meliana's umbra, an echo of her appears on the lancet, captured for posterity.

You killed me, it says. Her ghost looks younger than her body, a stubborn self-image fixated on what I'd guess she looked like a decade ago. *You* killed *me? You?*

"You had a knife to your grandson's throat," I say, as if I give a shit about Reeve after what he's pulled—but she was, as she said, an important person, and as I'm doing this at all, I might as well get things accurate. "Would you have hurt him to save yourself?"

Yes, says the umbra, utterly inflectionless.

"Killed him, even?"

Yes.

"That's why I killed you. To save his life."

A waste, says Meliana's ghost, though whether she means me or Reeve is anyone's guess.

A wave of dizziness swamps me. Staying upright takes a wrench of will, spots swimming before my vision. "Tell me, Meliana Cathan—how is the drug quartz made, and by who?"

And Meliana tells me. Ghosts can't lie, can't obfuscate. Her umbra shucks out all the secrets she kept in life, dispassionate as an invoice. At some point, Reeve staggers against the nearest wall and slumps to the ground, staring dumbly at his grandmother's body. I ignore him, asking her ghost about quartz profits; about her plan to frame us for the murder of Assemblyman Vitho; about addicting or framing the miners; about the false riots we passed in Argos, what feels like a lifetime ago. My head swims, dizzy with blood and magic; it feels like there's more I ought to ask, more names I ought to press for, but it's getting hard to stay upright, and the umbra, taxed by my questioning, is starting to fade and flicker.

"That's enough," I say. "That's—done. We're done, Meliana."

I'm not done, says the umbra, lifting its chin like Meliana did in life. *I've work to do before dawn—*

And then it's gone, evaporated like dew. The coil and lancet hum in my hand and then go dark. I stare at my stolen tools, not sure what to do beyond putting them back in the satchel, which is harder than it ought to be: my hands are clumsy, and with a sudden, shuddering thump, I'm on my knees.

"Oh," I say, as I put a hand to where I'm bleeding. Everything feels wet and tacky. "Oh, that's not good."

I keel over backwards. I ought to hit stone, but instead there's something soft and warm, that gives a little *oof!* as it takes my weight.

"Snow, you mawk," mumbles Nixa, settling me in her lap. Her voice is a rasp, but her hand is soft where she brushes my hair from my eyes. "Who gave you leave for heroics, huh?"

I shake my head, not able to answer. "Gem," I croak. "Is Gem all right?"

"He'll live. We'll all live. Including you, all right?"

Stupidly, I think of the ghost we met in the tunnels. Kerrec Lore, was that his name? "I'm so tired, Nix."

"That's 'coz you're all worn out from being an idiot. Just hang in there, na?"

"I want the music back," I whisper, and then the world fades out in a wheel of stars.

⚚ XII ⚚

I WAKE IN an unfamiliar bed, tucked into softer, cleaner sheets than any I've ever slept in. My eyes are gritty and my muscles ache, but otherwise, the pain I'm expecting never comes. I blink at the ceiling—painted pale gold, or maybe it only seems that way in the sunlight pouring through a nearby window—and turn my head to find an unexpected figure watching me from a bedside chair.

"Hey, Snow," says Lark. "You look like shit."

"Fuck you," I manage.

Lark grins at me, and I grin back. "Where am I? What happened?" And then, in a sudden lurch of panic, "Gem. What happened to Gem and Nixa?"

"Easy!" says Lark, waving for me to lie back down. "They're fine, okay? You're in a private healing room at Kithani's temple in Juno."

"Kithani's temple? But how—"

"Shh. Just let me tell it, yeah?" And she promptly proceeds to do so, a thoroughly Larkish summary of events I can't remember and for which she wasn't present. "When you passed out, Nixa yelled at that Reeve fel to get you help or she'd have his balls, so off he ran back to that Assemblyman you were meant to be foxing for in the first place, and *he* got you a rescari. Nixa hung around long enough to get clear-headed and to make sure you'n Gem were stable, then slunk off back to Charybdis—better that than dealing with goldplates anyday, hah!—but as she's a kindly sort of jake, she tipped me to what had happened so's I could come round you up.

"Well, I got here quick as quick—you know I've got my ins with the temples—and just in time, too, on account of Gem was all woke up and ready to kill Reeve right there on the Assemblyman's floor! I managed to talk him down from that, at least for now, and got 'em all talking about what to do with that ghost you captured. Kithani's tits, Snow!" She whistles, the sound two-toned as always from her missing tooth. "That's some foxfucking brass and no mistake. Well, of course that Vitho fel wants to take it straight to the Assembly, only Gem wants to make sure that something actually comes of it and it doesn't get buried, yeah? What with how you risked your lives to get it. Which is why you're lucky that I was there, 'coz as it happens, I know a vox over in Ushai's temple, so I say to them, let's make a copy! And nobody can argue with that, so that's what happens: Gem gets one copy and Vitho the other, and meanwhile—I should've said, sorry—all those bodies you left behind are getting cleaned up and it's nearly dawn, right? Only everything's gonna get messy soon, which means it's not safe for anyone to stay at the Assemblyman's place, so Reeve fucks off to wherever—"

I snort at that, unable to help myself. Lark looks pleased with us both, and continues: "—and Gem goes, too, to let the Red Steps know what happened, and show them his

copy, and also to tell them that Reeve's a fucking ass of a
snitch, apparently, and not to be trusted. And all the time
you were still passed out, so me'n the rescari who fixed
you—Siva, her name is, she seems all right—we brought
you back here to rest up—it's on the Assemblyman's coin,
so don't fuss about that—and, well. Now you're awake!
Oh, and don't worry about getting back to Charybdis;
it's always easier going downgate than up, but I've got
some dye for your hair and I'm organising a gatepass, just
in case. And clean clothes, too." She wrinkles her nose.
"Believe me, you need them. Though you're clean enough
now; the dedicates gave you a wash while you were out of it."

"They washed me?" I say, fixing on what seems like the
easiest thing to deal with.

"Yes, yes. Don't worry; I supervised. The whole thing
was very medicinal."

"Good. That's good to know." I shut my eyes, trying
to let it all sink in. "And Gem," I say, when I think I can
trust my voice again. "Is he, I mean—is he here?"

"He's not," says Lark, and the pity in her voice is a
kindly knife. "But that's not—Snow. When he saw how
bad you were hurt… that hurt him, too, I think."

"Sure," I say, and turn my face to the wall. "Of course."

"I'll get you some food," Lark says, a beat later.
"Though if you're still tired, rest. Kithani knows, you'll
need it!"

I nod dumbly against the pillow, listening as Lark rises
and leaves. I feel hollow, worse in a way than I did coming
down from quartz. Does Gem not want to see me again?
He'd be here if he wanted to be; I know him well enough
to know that much. I think back to the argument we
had in the terrestri tunnel, wincing at my mawkishness.
Why would he stick around? He's got his own life, his
own cause. I helped him for a time, and now it's done. It
shouldn't hurt more than losing him the first time did.
What wound runs eight years deep?

I fall asleep without meaning to, and when I wake, there's food on a tray with a note from Lark, saying she's gone to get my gatepass. I eat; it's good, but I barely taste it. Is that from the quartz or something else? I strip and piss in the washroom, staring at myself in the glass: I've always been all muscle and bone, but more of the latter is visible than I'd like to see, and the thick, fresh scar on my lower back is shiny and tender to the touch. I find the dye Lark mentioned—dark brown or black, I'm not sure which—and wet my hair to help it sink in. The echo-Snow in the glass looks alien, dark-haired enough to pass for normal. I look away and put on the clean new clothes Lark left—all black and a size too big, I've no idea where she found them, but including a pair of gloves that fit, to hide my silver fingers— and, with nothing else to do, I go back to bed and wait.

I doze again, but wake at the sound of Lark's return. She eyes me up approvingly and asks if I'm ready to go.

"I am," I say. I was ready before we got here, but I don't want to seem ungrateful, so I keep my mouth shut and let her talk for both of us as she leads me out, away from the private hospice rooms and into the temple proper.

Outside, the sun beams down on the city, bright and sharp as lyracite. The dazzle hurts my eyes; I'm still feeling a little unsteady, but I shove it away as Lark links our arms and leads me on through Juno Precinct, cutting a path through healthier, more vibrant crowds than any found in Charybdis. Sourness stirs my gut. Shouldn't I want this for everyone? I do, I do, but I don't know if I believe it's possible; not in New Arcadia. Maybe Meliana's ghost will help things change, or maybe it won't. It's the walls that matter, Jerichae's walls and our inheritance. So long as they stand, the city will suffer, and even if you knocked them down, the shadow of them would stay. That's a long, hard thing to fix, and I can't see the end of it.

But maybe that's my failing. Maybe my heart's as numb as my other nerveless flesh, and that's why Gem is gone.

It doesn't matter. Charybdis is in me down to the bone, and even if I didn't owe two deaths to Savu Scapegrace, I can't fathom living anywhere else. The shadow of the walls is long and deep. Where else am I to live?

Another time, I might care to marvel at all the new sights around me, but not today. Today, I let Lark lead me like a simpleton, past gates and guards, through a rickshaw ride, and all of it unremarkable. What a difference it makes, to be seen as other than what I am! I dig gloved nails into my gloved palm and try not to scream at everything for being kind to a version of me that doesn't exist.

By the time we make it back to Charybdis, the sun has started to dip and exhaustion is reasserting itself. Lark bids me farewell with a kiss on the cheek and a worried look in her mismatched eyes, one blue, one brown.

"Take care, Snow," she says, and pushes something into my hand. I stare at it, uncomprehending. "That's your fee," she says, after an awkward moment. "Gem's fee. Remember?"

Numb. I want to be numb. "Of course," I say, and shove it into my pocket.

I'm two blocks away before I think to ask what became of my shockjack. Confiscated by the Assemblyman, probably; they're not exactly legal, and the damage I wrought on Meliana's guards is why. I wonder if I killed them all, or only the one whose neck I broke. I can't make myself care either way.

I reach my front door and shove it open. I never bother to lock it: everyone nearby knows who I am, and even if they didn't, I've nothing of value worth stealing. Sohlan's old house is two narrow stories, crammed in a row of similar buildings like crooked teeth crowding out a jaw. Kitchen, pantry and a tiny parlour downstairs; bedroom and bathroom upstairs. I kick off my boots, angrily satisfied by how loudly they thunk on the warped wooden floors, and trudge up the rickety stairs. I've thought about getting drunk, but I don't want to be around people right now. All I want is rest.

I turn the corner and freeze.

Gem's standing in my bedroom.

For several long seconds, neither of us speaks or moves. My pulse lights up like the lancet did when I held it to Meliana's ghost.

"I'm sorry," Gem says, before I can say anything. "I'm sorry I wasn't there when you woke. It was cowardly of me."

"What?" I say. *Cowardly? How does that make sense?*

"You saw me on quartz," says Gem, hands flexing at his sides. He looks away, jaw working as he swallows. "You saw me beg. I thought… I don't know what I thought. But I was ashamed all the same. Am ashamed." He drew a ragged breath. "I can still—it's still *in* me, the itch for it. Like a tooth in need of pulling. Some days I think of it even without this want, this *need*, but now—" He looks away. "I am ashamed," he whispers. "Ashamed of how easily I might slip, even knowing better. I don't want to—gods alone know, I don't want to go back to that—but the way I felt this morning, it took everything in me not go haring off to beg for one last dose, just one, to chase the aches away."

I step closer to him, heart in my throat. "There's no shame in that, Gem. That you gave it up at all—that says more about you than anything else." And then, because his confession gives a shape to some of the wrongness I've felt since morning, "I've wanted it, too, I think. In flashes, since I woke up again. Like a hunger, or a hollowness, here." I touch a hand to my abdomen. "I've tried not to think about it, but I know what it is, and I hate that it's there but it's not—it wasn't our doing, Gem. Not yours, not mine. It was Reeve and his fucking grandmother, and every other goldplate bastard who's thought to profit from misery."

Gem nods, drifting close enough to touch. His proximity panics me, like moths beneath my skin.

"The Red Steps," I blurt, cheeks heating. "You—Lark said you took a copy of the ghost to them?"

"I did," says Gem.."They've struck an accord with Vitho; he's got ten days to make his copy public through official channels, and if he doesn't, then the Red Steps will do it for him."

"And do you think he'll—"

"I don't know," says Gem—too quickly, cutting me off. He winces at himself. "I don't know," he says again, more softly. "After all this, I want to believe that something good will come of the truth, but things are rarely so simple, and the way things are in Argos... there's going to be blood, Snow. No matter who goes public first, there's going to be blood; the connexi will see to that, and the Guild, and the goldplates. But some of it will be theirs, and maybe it has to be, for things to change."

I think of what I did to Tamek; the truce I built from his death. Some plants thrive best when fed on blood and bone, and perhaps change is, too, but all things which eat must be seeded first, and if you spread gore on barren soil, the only thing you'll reap is a charnel-house. Time alone will tell if Meliana's ghost is seed enough—time and the hard, sharp work without which hope stays weightless, a shadow of action instead of the thing that casts it. Whatever happens next, there will be more to do—but for now, in this house, there's only me and Gem, and as he takes my quartz-fingered hand, the last wall between us crumbles.

"Snow," he says, eyes dark as he looks me over. "Are you—you're all right, otherwise?"

"I'm all right," I say, though all at once I can barely breathe. "I thought you didn't want me, because—" I force myself to meet his gaze, "—because of Reeve."

Gem winces at that, but doesn't let me go. "Reeve was safe," he says, dark laughter edging the words. "I knew he was no type of duke, to be at risk of wanting me back, and he was—is—nothing like you, Snow."

His voice goes raw in a way that makes my heart clench. "He wasn't *you*, d'you understand? Nobody could be. Eight years, I kept waiting to want something, anything else, but it never took, and I'd *killed* you. Except somehow, it turns out I didn't."

"Gem—"

He leans in, clasping the nape of my neck to press our foreheads together, tilting me up as he tips himself down, and after a moment he drops my hand in favour of cupping my face.

"Snow," he says, and I could weep at the tenderness of it. I laugh instead, alight and crazy and full of something that's almost hope—not for the city or its future, but for me alone. "Snow, can I know you again? Do you—would you want to know me?"

"I've never stopped," I say, voice wet, and twine my arms around him.

About the Author

Foz Meadows is a queer fantasy author, essayist, reviewer and poet; their work has been published in venues such as *Apex Magazine*, *Goblin Fruit* and *The Huffington Post*. They are a four-time Hugo Award nominee for Best Fan Writer, which they won in 2019; they also won the 2017 Ditmar Award for Best Fan Writer, for which they are a three-time nominee. In 2017, their portal fantasy *An Accident of Stars* was a finalist for the Bisexual Book Awards, and in 2018, their queer Shakespearean novella *Coral Bones* won the Norma K. Hemming Award in the short fiction category. Their most recent novel, *A Strange and Stubborn Endurance*, is a queer romantic fantasy published by Tor; the sequel, *All the Hidden Paths*, is due for release in December 2023.

About the Press

Neon Hemlock is a Washington, DC-based small press publishing speculative fiction, rad zines, and queer chapbooks. Publishers Weekly once called us "the apex of queer speculative fiction publishing" and we're still beaming. Learn more about us at neonhemlock.com and on social medias at @neonhemlock.